GHOST MESSAGES

ENVIRONMENTAL BENEFITS STATEMENT

Coteau Books saved the following resources by printing the pages of this book on chlorine free paper made with 100% post-consumer waste.

TREES	WATER	SOLID WASTE	GREENHOUSE GASES
22	**14,883**	**1,883**	**4,891**
FULLY GROWN	GALLONS	POUNDS	POUNDS

 Calculation based on the methodological framework of Paper Calculator 2.0 - EDF

MIX
Paper from responsible sources
FSC® C103214
www.fsc.org

GHOST MESSAGES

JACQUELINE GUEST

www.coteaubooks.com

This novel is a work of fiction. Names, characters, places, and incidents either are the product of the author's imagination or are used fictitiously. Any resemblance to actual persons, living or dead, is coincidental.

Edited by Laura Peetoom
Design by Tania Craan
Typeset by Susan Buck
Printed and bound in Canada by Houghton Boston

Library and Archives Canada Cataloguing in Publication

Guest, Jacqueline
      Ghost messages / Jacqueline Guest.

ISBN 978-1-55050-458-3

      1. Great Eastern (Steamship)--Juvenile fiction. I. Title.

PS8563.U365G56 2011   jC813'.54   C2010-907596-X

Library of Congress Control Number: 2011921840

2517 Victoria Avenue
Regina, Saskatchewan
Canada   S4P 0T2
www.coteaubooks.com

10 9 8 7 6 5 4 3 2

Available in Canada from:
Publishers Group Canada
2440 Viking Way
Richmond, British Columbia
Canada V6V 1N2

Available in the US from:
Orca Book Publishers
www.orcabook.com
1-800-210-5277

Coteau Books gratefully acknowledges the financial support of its publishing program by: the Saskatchewan Arts Board, the Canada Council for the Arts, the Government of Canada through the Canada Book Fund, the Government of Saskatchewan through the Creative Economy Entrepreneurial Fund and the City of Regina Arts Commission.

For Gordon with love

and

*to the real Eilish, a wild Irish lass with
true fire and a wicked sense of humour.*

MYSTERY MAN

"MAGIC AWAITS HERE!" CRIED THE SKELETAL MAN AS he held up a bony hand. "Fortunes told by a thirteen-year-old girl born with the second sight – the seventh daughter of a seventh daughter! One touch and Madame Ailish will lift the veil to give you a glimpse of the unknown!" He waved his shillelagh at an ancient wooden caravan. "Step right up!"

Inside the wagon, Ailish O'Connor straightened the colourful gypsy scarf tied around her long auburn hair and swiped at a crumb of cheese that had fallen onto the crystal ball from her hastily eaten supper.

"Seventh daughter of a seventh daughter, my fanny," she grumbled. "If only. At least then I'd have some help around here."

It was getting on to evening and more light would be needed for the next tarot card reading. She lit the coal-oil lantern, the wick flaring to brilliant life; then turned it down to make the atmosphere more mysterious for her next client. They seemed to expect it, though Ailish could have helped them just as much in an open field at noonday.

Ailish and her father were here in Valentia on Foilhummerum Bay to join in the festivities celebrating the voyage of the *Great Eastern*, the mighty ship that had the daunting task of laying the first transatlantic telegraph cable. Her da's passion was ships and this one was like no other in the entire world.

The undersea cable would join Europe and North America with almost instantaneous communication. Ailish imagined sending a message from here on the west coast of Ireland and having it received all the way across the ocean, in Newfoundland off the east coast of Canada, all in the wink of an eye. Now that was magic!

And Ireland could use something wonderful. Times were still hard, even years after the Great Potato Famine that had starved a million people. Her father, who could always see the bright side of things, when Ailish doubted such a side existed, struggled ceaselessly to make ends meet. She saw how the constant battle wore him down and because she loved him so much, she tried to ignore the irritating things he did – like going to the local tavern and leaving her to deal with the customers alone, as he had done earlier today.

As Ailish waited, she watched an industrious brown spider spin its web in an arching corner of the caravan's ceiling, but no one seeking answers appeared at the door. Standing, she stretched the kinks out of her back and addressed the busy bug. "If my customers only knew that I truly can see mysterious things, they'd appreciate my advice more. Maybe then I could raise my fee and we wouldn't have to worry on how to pay for our next meal."

Only one living person took Ailish seriously, and that was Uncle Peter. He was not really her uncle, simply a family friend, and, if you wanted to get fancy about it, his proper title was Sir Peter Fitzgerald, the Knight of Kerry. As the ruling authority in this part of Ireland, he was an important man to be sure, but Uncle Peter did take her uncanny talent seriously and always listened intently to whatever she revealed. He was her favourite customer and paid handsomely for her readings.

Clambering onto a wobbly twig chair, she pushed open the small window set high in the curved wooden wall and peered out.

It was late but there were still people about. Not long ago, the scene would have warmed her soul – the turf fires smouldering, their peaty scent earthy and comforting, as the music of the fiddlers washed over her like a bright and bubbly tide. But now, it was different. Now she had no mother to share the pleasant evening with.

Early stars poked holes in the indigo canopy overhead and let dazzling pinpoints of light peep through. With a familiar pang, Ailish wondered if her ma was looking down through those tiny portals from heaven and missing them like Ailish missed her. It had been two long years since the fever took her and Ailish still ached. Tomorrow was July 23, 1865 – it would have been her mother's thirty-fifth birthday.

She saw her da and a burly stranger walking toward the wagon. He was probably some ne'er-do-well her father had met in the pub today. Lately, her da had taken to visiting more of the drinking establishments than usual. Every town they'd passed through, he'd find some excuse to leave her and then return hours later with never a word. This was no doubt the reason why their meagre store of hard-earned coins was now gone.

As she watched them approach, the tall man looked her way, and for an instant their eyes locked. Ailish took an involuntary step backward, slipping from her precarious perch and bumping the table with her crystal ball, nearly knocking it to the floor. She felt unexpectedly flustered and fumbled with nervous fingers as she pulled off her scarf, then gathered her fortune-telling paraphernalia and tucked it into the small storage trunk.

Her father bustled into their cramped quarters, with the hulking newcomer filling the doorway behind him.

"Ailish, me darlin'," he began, making a grand gesture with his arm, "Meet Rufus Dalton, a gent and a scholar. He's from the mighty *Great Eastern* and is here for a wee drink and a chin wag."

He flashed her one of his devilish smiles and Ailish knew this would be a late night.

"*Failte*, welcome, Mr. Dalton." Ailish reached out to shake hands.

The second their fingers touched an icy black serpent slithered down her spine. She recoiled. This man carried a terrible darkness with him!

Ailish snatched her hand from Dalton's grasp, hiding it behind her back. She turned to her father to see if he'd caught her reaction, but he still had that silly smile tattooed to his face. She wiggled her brows and slid her eyes toward the stranger, but her father was oblivious. What good did it do to have a daughter with the second sight, if you were so daft that you ignored the warning signs she sent? They could be in mortal danger.

"Something wrong?" the big man growled, his words thick with a coarse English accent.

Maybe she was overreacting. Maybe she was simply tired. She sighed as an overpowering weariness wrapped her in its worn cloak. Perhaps this stranger was merely one more crooked sailor, a brigand – ports were full of them.

"Ach, no sir, just a night chill. I'll fling a chunk of turf on the fire." She went to the creel and busied herself stoking the potbellied stove with the peat they used to ward off the damp.

"Fetch the whiskey, Ails, me girl, and a couple of glasses." Her da took off his coat and tossed it onto the chest of drawers they shared before lowering himself into the rickety chair she'd nearly fallen from moments before.

Ailish noted he used her nickname, knowing this was his way of trying to get on her good side when it came to his drink, which she regarded as a weakness. She avoided eye contact with the stranger and did as she was told.

Retrieving her favourite book, the one about a monster brought to life by a mad doctor, Ailish settled back against the thin wooden partition that separated the common room from her sleeping area. Peeking over the book, she saw her father pour generous dollops of the fiery amber liquid into the cracked glasses, then give one to Dalton.

"*Slainte!* Good health!" Her da took a long gulp of his drink before going on enthusiastically. "This transatlantic cable is a grand adventure, to be sure, and I've heard miraculous things about the ship."

"Aye, that be right," Dalton agreed, taking a small sip. "The world is filled with many seafaring marvels, but the *Great Eastern* remains the most fantastic of all. Why, she's five times bigger than any ship afloat!"

"'The Wonder of the Seas,' they call her." Ailish's father took another deep draught of his drink.

Dalton nodded. "And she carries fifteen thousand tons of coal, enough to sail near round the world without refueling. The *Great Eastern* is the exact right vessel for laying this cable."

Listening to this, Ailish rolled her eyes. You'd think the two of them had single-handedly built the blasted boat, they sounded so full of themselves.

Although the visitor's glass was still half full, her father refilled it and his own, spilling a little onto the faded tablecloth in his haste. "Coal, you say, but I heard she was a sailing ship?"

Dalton nodded, swirling the whiskey in the glass. "She has six masts and enough canvas to cover a small village, but she also has a screw propeller and giant paddle-wheels on either side which is why nothing stops her."

Ailish went back to her book while the two men continued talking and drinking. The heat from the stove made her drowsy, and she'd almost dozed off when the sound of her name roused her.

"Ach, Ails, you've got this place as hot as Hades." Her father wiped his forehead with a handkerchief, then removed his colourful orange striped vest, the one her ma had sewn for his birthday, and carefully draped it over the back of his chair. "Ailish is the apple of me eye, Rufus. She has the second sight, you know. Famous, she is."

He beamed with pride, but Ailish was tired and thoughts of her ungrateful customers leapt to her lips. "For all the good it's done us. We're poor as church mice."

"Now, now my girl, you've helped many souls and that's no lie." Her father chided gently, his speech slightly slurred.

Ailish's temper flared with the peat. "I work hard to help these folks but to them it's all sham, a penny's entertainment, and we end up spending our lives drudging around in this infernal caravan and eating champ!" The thought of another meal of boiled potatoes made her stomach gurgle unpleasantly.

"I know it's been hard since your ma died, Ails."

When he mentioned her mother, her da found something interesting to look at in the bottom of his glass, avoiding Ailish's gaze, and she felt guilty. She knew how much her mother's death had pained him too. "But your ma would be proud if she knew you were keeping up the family tradition with your fey gift. Besides, me darlin', we won't be doin' this for long. I'm that close to makin' our dream come true." He winked at her before turning to their visitor.

"We'll be living with my brother Seamus in Heart's Content, Newfoundland once this cable's laid. He's what you call a telegrapher, and a fine one if his letters are to be believed."

Ailish cleared her throat loudly, interrupting her da before he divulged any more private details to this stranger. "I'm sure Mr. Dalton doesn't need to hear our family plans."

But he charged on, oblivious to her hint. "Yes, sir, sixteen hundred miles across the Atlantic, that's where the Canadian end of this miraculous cable will surface, and that's where we'll be if everything works out the way I've planned. We'll be buying a fine fishing boat and a grand house to live in. Ah, 'twill be amazing, it will."

Her patience at an end and exhausted from her long day, Ailish couldn't listen to that old story once more or she'd scream. "Da, I'm too tired for any of your fairy tales and we shouldn't be discussing this in public." She threw a silencing glare at her bleary-eyed father, but he resolutely shook his head.

"It's not blarney, Ails. It will happen. Why do you think I've been scouring the taverns from here to Belfast? Not for the drink, to be sure. I've not a shilling for that. I've been looking for a buyer for a very special trinket. Soon, we'll be having it all, lass, and I'll prove it to you."

The news her father hadn't been squandering their money on whiskey came as a surprise and a relief to Ailish. But where, then, had their savings gone?

Tilting slightly, her da stood, then lurched to the potato basket and rummaged in it. She wondered what he was up to as he straightened unsteadily and held out a small bundle of dusty sackcloth. "This is going to make our dream come true."

Carefully, he unwrapped the mystery parcel and Ailish gasped as the soft lantern light glinted off a tiny statue of a golden horse. Diamond eyes dazzled and the intricately braided silver bridle was anchored with small fiery rubies. She gazed at the figurine.

"Is it real?" she breathed, spellbound.

"Right out of the palace at St. Petersburg. I bought this off of a Russian soldier boy who was fleeing the czar and needed money, any money. It cost me more than I wanted to part with – two pounds, which was all our hard earned savings – but I've been around a wee while and could see the value in this golden filly." He chuckled. "Your Uncle Peter laughed when I showed him the bill of sale. He said it was worth a small fortune and would replace our savings a hundred times over. We'd be set for life. And he told me we'd have no trouble selling it, the thing's that fine. Once we're done here, we're going to Dublin. Rufus says he'll introduce me to a merchant who'll buy this, and then it's off to Newfoundland for us."

Boots scraped on the rough wooden floor and both Ailish and her father turned to the brooding stranger who listened so quietly.

She swallowed. There was something about this man that made her afraid and she knew her da should never even have told him about this treasure, much less brought it out in front of him.

Dalton's eyes narrowed into slits that reminded Ailish of a lizard. She shuddered, feeling as if someone was shovelling dirt onto her grave. The look on her father's face told Ailish he, too, was having second thoughts about the man he'd chosen to help him sell his fabulous statue. Flustered, he hastily re-wrapped the tiny gilt horse in the sacking and stuffed it back into the basket.

"Ach, but that's business that can wait for tomorrow." He tossed the words off lightly, as though what he'd shown her was nothing at all. "Now, off to bed with ye and no more foolish talk."

Ailish nodded mutely and retreated to her cramped sleeping area, closing the door. Her head was filled with questions. Why hadn't her da told her about this sooner? She wouldn't have nagged him so much about his frequent trips to every village watering hole if she'd known the why of it.

As she lay listening to the murmur of voices, she couldn't stop wondering if the statue had been genuine. Or was it just sparkle and shine, with no substance? It seemed too amazing to be true, but if it was real... Oh, if it was real, then this would indeed be the end of the leprechaun's rainbow for them, and just a short hop to Newfoundland!

— • — • —

GLASS SHARDS RAINED FROM THE SKY AND STRUCK THE roof of the caravan in a crystal storm. Other sounds drifted into Ailish's dream – scuffling, bumping and thumping. Groggily, she dragged herself out of a leaden sleep.

The noises continued, but more loudly now and she could hear cursing. Ailish was fully awake in an instant. Throwing back the covers, she leapt out of her warm bed and yanked open the sleeping room door.

The sight that met her eyes made her breath come in small, feathery gasps. Her father lay on the floor, a halo of crimson blood around his head. She couldn't tear her eyes away from the sticky red stain as it soaked into the worn wooden planks.

The potato basket lay tipped on its side, the contents scattered. Rufus Dalton was nowhere to be seen.

"Da!" Ailish cried. She rushed to her father's side, terrified of what she would find.

His skin was ghostly white as blood continued to seep from the jagged gash on his head. Tears pooled in Ailish's eyes and her mother's dead face swam in those tears – the same still, pale look that her father had now.

"You can't die, da. You can't!" She had to do something, but what? Then she remembered Mrs. Murphy in the wagon next to theirs. The widow woman was a midwife and knew some doctoring.

Her father groaned as his eyes fluttered, then opened. Weakly, he held up the scrap of sackcloth. "The blagger took the golden horse…" he rasped. "Ails, he took our future."

Rage boiled up like liquid fire; then a wave of guilt hit Ailish, extinguishing the flames. She'd known Rufus Dalton was evil. She should have done something more, made her father listen. She, of all people, should have heeded her feelings, but no, she'd ignored the warning and now her dear, sweet father had paid the price.

She heard the pain in his voice and wondered if it was because of the blow on his head or the loss of the wonderful statue. Either way, it was up to her to fix the problem. She owed him that.

"Don't you worry about your treasure, Da. I'll get it back."

And as Ailish ran for help, she vowed she would.

2

SECRET MESSAGE

.... --- .-- -- .. -.-. .... -- --- -. .-..-- -.- .. -. .- .-- ..- ..- .-- ..... .- ....

AILISH WASN'T SURE SHE WAS DOING THE RIGHT THING leaving her injured father with Mrs. Murphy, but if she were going to find Dalton, she had to act fast. Pulling her paisley shawl over her head to ward off the chill, she ran through the pre-dawn darkness to the dock. She had to stop the low dog before he made it back to his ship.

Rounding a tall stack of crates, she saw an early morning dockworker busily writing on a piece of paper. "Excuse me, sir," she asked, her breathing laboured from her run. "Have ye seen a bloke called Rufus Dalton? My da sent me to give him a message."

"You're too late, miss." He nodded in the direction of the harbour.

Ailish looked to the sea and there, silhouetted by the thin strip of pink dawn light, a small ship steamed out of the bay. She knew it would be the ferry to the huge cable-laying ship, docked far out in the bay because of its size.

"Oh no, no, *no!*" she wailed, watching as her quarry slipped like quicksilver from her grasp. "He can't get away this easily!"

Concern at her plea was plain on the sailor's face as he tried to reassure her. "Come now, don't fret, lass. I work on the *Great Eastern* and will be taking these last crates out to her before we sail. Tell me your message and I'll give it to Dalton when I see him." His rich Irish brogue was warm and friendly.

Ailish shook her head dejectedly. "Don't trouble yourself, sir. You were right, it's too late." She turned and slowly walked away.

She'd failed. It was her fault her father had been hurt and now she had to tell him she'd let their hope for the future sail away.

Climbing atop one of the wooden crates, Ailish sat and tried to think of what to do next. She had to get that statue back, but how? As she wiggled trying to get more comfortable, the rough wood snagged her pantalets tearing a small hole in the undergarment. She pulled her dress further down to hide the tiny embarrassment and as she did so, the lid wobbled. The crate must not be nailed shut.

Jumping off, she pushed on the heavy cover and managed to move it enough to look inside. The crate held bits and bobs of machinery, but there was enough room for a thin girl to hide within. She smiled as a crazy idea flashed into her mind.

She'd follow Dalton to the ship; then while they were unloading the cargo, she'd find the statue, steal it back, and return to shore with the ferry before anyone was the wiser.

Checking to make sure the dockworker was busy, Ailish clambered into the large box, sliding the lid back into place behind her. A crack in her wooden canopy let a tiny sliver of early morning light into the crowded compartment and the smell of the fresh salt air had a tang to it. If this crate was going to the *Great Eastern*, then so was she.

Yawning, she settled in to wait.

— - • — —

AILISH AWOKE WITH A START. RUBBING HER EYES, SHE uncurled and tried to stretch her cramped muscles.

The air smelled differently now. She caught a whiff of oil and the bite of metal. She must already be aboard the ship, which meant it was time to find Rufus Dalton and the treasure. Struggling to her knees, Ailish reached over her head and pushed on the lid.

It wouldn't move.

She pushed again, but still the stubborn wood refused to budge.

Fear prickled her scalp as she looked up. No splinter of light showed through the rough-hewn boards. Furtively searching, she found an empty knothole in the side of the crate. Pressing her eye to the opening, Ailish peered out.

She was indeed in the *Great Eastern's* cavernous hold

surrounded by stacks of boxes in all sizes and shapes. But if there was no light coming through the lid, that could mean only one thing – another crate was piled on top of hers.

She was trapped!

Should she call out? Who would hear? And if they did rescue her, she knew they'd send her back to shore before she had a chance to find what she'd come for. The thought of Dalton getting away made her hold her tongue. She'd wait a while at least, and hope someone came to move the top crate and free her from this wooden prison.

Time crawled painfully past while she listened to the clangs and bangs as the ship was loaded.

Finally, Ailish could wait no longer. She had to use the privy and that meant getting out of her wooden nest before she had a mortifying accident. If she had to give herself away, so be it. At that moment, she heard footsteps loudly clomping down metal stairs and then coming toward her across the iron floor. Panic seized her. Was it Dalton? After what he'd done to her father, she knew he was capable of terrible violence.

Carefully, she put her eye to the knothole, afraid of whom she'd discover on the other side.

Relief bubbled up like soapsuds. It was the same kind sailor from the dock. Ailish scrunched her eyes and reached out with her mind. She felt no darkness, no shadows from this man which was a very good thing as there was no choice. She had to call to him for help.

Ailish wasn't sure how she'd explain being bunged up in that crate, but something would come to her. Taking a deep breath, she opened her mouth to yell, when a bone-racking shiver sliced down her back, freezing the air in her lungs.

Another set of footsteps was approaching.

"Well, if it isn't Paddy Whelan. I've been lookin' for you."

The growl was unmistakable. This time, it *was* Rufus Dalton.

Ailish peeked through her spy hole. The man Dalton addressed was her rescuer. Paddy Whelan, a fine Irish name! She felt as if they were friends already.

"Who told you to come down here?" the Englishman asked tersely.

"That's a good question," Paddy replied. "I received a message, an unsigned note telling me to go below and stow this more securely." He stepped forward; there was a scraping sound and a shaft of light slid through the crack in the lid of Ailish's hideaway. "Someone was worried it would fall over and smash if we hit rough water. They must not know much about this ship." Paddy set the crate he was holding into an empty corner, then started back toward the stairs.

"Wait right there, sailor." Dalton took one long stride, reached out a meaty hand and spun Paddy around. "I'm cable crew chief and I'll tell you when you can go."

From her secret vantage point, Ailish saw Paddy's jaw

muscles tighten in a very distinct way. If the man had hackles, they would have been up.

"I found out a couple of interesting things about you." Dalton's fleshy lips sneered. "You brought a lot of money on board this ship, eighty pounds, to be precise."

Ailish sucked in her breath. Eighty pounds! Besides Uncle Peter, this made Paddy Whelan the richest Irishman she'd ever met. If she and her da had that kind of money, they could have gone to Newfoundland and lived like kings, or maybe a king and a princess.

Paddy's eyes grew wide with astonishment. "How do you know that?"

Dalton snorted. "The captain may be the boss above decks, but make no mistake, down below, I run this ship. One of my lads overheard you tell the purser about the cash when you had him lock it in the safe."

"That money is for my family." Paddy said defensively. "I sold our land in Ireland and we're going to make a fresh start in Canada."

"I'd say that may be tough to do once I show the captain this…"

As Ailish watched, Dalton held up a copy of the *London Illustrated News*. The outsize headline read "Fenian Traitors Plan To Wreck Transatlantic Cable!"

"If anything were to happen to the cable now, everyone will know an Irishman's to blame and this will show them which lying dog it was." Dalton pointed to the large picture under the headline and Paddy leaned forward to peer at it closely.

"That's rubbish! I'm not a Fenian!" he protested indignantly. "I was at the meeting, yes, because the Fenians wish a free Ireland and so do I. I went to listen, but when they started talking violence, I wanted no part of it. That picture was taken moments before I left."

"It looks like proof of a plot to me. If I show Captain Anderson, he'll throw you in the brig to make sure nothing happens to his precious cable, and then he'll turn you over to the police when we reach Newfoundland. They'll lock you up and hire a hangman." The corners of Dalton's mouth turned up in a sly smile. "Or we could do a private deal and the captain need never see this."

"Why, you rotten... You'll not get that eighty pounds! It's all the money my family has." Paddy took a menacing step toward Dalton, who stumbled backward in his haste to avoid the angry sailor.

"Back off, Whelan! I told you, belowdecks I run this ship, and you could end up having a little accident."

"Don't threaten me, Dalton. Do what you must. I won't give you one farthing." Paddy spun on his heel and stalked away.

Dalton watched him leave before following at a safe distance.

Ailish wasn't sure what to make of their argument, but did know she now had a chance to follow the low-life thief who had stolen her treasure. She shoved on the crude wooden lid. With a groan of protest, it slid open and she hopped out, pushing it back into place behind her.

Trying not to make any noise on the cold iron floor, she hurried toward the stairs. With a little luck, she could catch up with Dalton and hopefully, he'd lead her to the fabulous horse.

She'd reached the bottom stair when she heard men's voices coming from above.

Looking around, Ailish frantically tried to find someplace to take cover. Her crate was far across the hold and she'd never have time to crawl back in without the sailors seeing her.

"Over here! Hurry, miss!" The command came to her from behind several large wooden barrels that were stacked beside the stairs.

Surprised, Ailish stopped, unsure she'd heard right.

"Come on!" the voice urged again, this time, with a distinct note of irritation.

Peering into the darkness, she tried to see who'd spoken. Should she trust this unknown rescuer? She had to. There was no time to investigate if whoever owned this mystery voice would be any more dangerous than the men coming. She darted for the barrels and squeezed herself into the small space behind them.

A boy about her age, with curly dark hair and a mischievous look about him, squatted there. Hoping she was doing the right thing, she squished herself beside him.

Together, Ailish and her new ally watched as two

gruff looking men climbed down the stairs then strode over to the very crate she'd been hiding in and wrenched the lid off. She gulped.

They lifted out several machine parts then replaced the lid, nailing it shut before leaving.

Ailish couldn't believe it. If it hadn't been for this stranger, she would have run right into the sailors on the stairs, or worse, they would have found her cowering in the wooden box.

3
STOWAWAY!

"I OWE YOU MY GRATITUDE, SIR. THEY ALMOST HAD ME."
Ailish stood, then eased out from behind the casks and
dusted the dirt off her dress. She was in a rather awkward
spot. "I suppose you're wondering why I'm here ..." She
couldn't think of anything to say and decided to turn the
tables instead. "But since you were stuck behind the barrels too, perhaps you'd tell me why you had to avoid those
men and who you are?"

She waited as the boy finished wiggling free of their
mutual hiding place. He was dressed differently from the
lads she knew. The sleeves on his shirt were loose-fitting
and his pants were tied off above the calf. She was about
to comment on his sailor's garb, when he looked at her
and the words dried up.

He had the strangest eyes. They were large and lumi-
nous and ocean-green.

"I was hanging about down here, like always, and the
vibration in the deck plates told me we were about to have
company. I figured from watching you climb out of that

crate that you didn't want anyone to know you were aboard so I thought I'd help a damsel in distress. The name's David Jones, but you can call me Davy." In the light from the gas lamps, his strange eyes sparked like lightning bugs. "I work here. I'm a bash boy."

"A bash boy? What's that?" Ailish had never heard the term before, but from his accent, she could tell he was from England; maybe it was some peculiar thing known only to the English.

"Hear that?" Davy asked, cocking an ear.

At that moment, Ailish heard a distant clang of a hammer striking metal.

"That's Charlie." Davy explained. "He's a riveter here on the ship and I'm his helper. I hold the hot bolts while Charlie smashes them in. We keep the ship, and all three million of her rivets, from falling apart," he added proudly.

"Oh, my goodness! That does sound impressive," she said with genuine respect.

"Who are these 'Fenians' Dalton was going on about?"

His question caught her by surprise. She couldn't ignore it, but gabbing about the Fenians was not something any Irishman did. Ailish tried to explain. "We, that is the Irish, don't like being ruled by the English. It chafes every Irishman who draws breath. The Fenians are the brave souls who speak out for independence but they've been branded traitors for their efforts. They're hunted, and when caught, the gallows await. We common folk agree with these freedom fighters but because of the severe penalties, the only grumblings you'll hear are those muttered where the authorities can't hear. An Irishman's loyalty to Her Majesty can never waver..." She paused. "At least not within earshot of an Englishman."

It suddenly struck her that this bash boy was English and perhaps she'd said too much. He could turn her in for speaking such thoughts!

Instead, he nodded sagely. "Being captain of your own ship makes sense to me. I'd sign on too."

Ailish immediately liked Davy, even though, for some odd reason, she got no *feeling* about him, whether good or bad. He could be Satan in a pink bonnet for all she could sense.

"So what are you doing on my ship?" Davy asked bluntly.

"Ah, actually, the reason I'm aboard is because..." Ailish groped for some way to explain her presence. "Because I'm visiting my uncle, my *favourite* uncle," she amended. "He's a sailor and well, I guess I wandered off and ended up here. I was afraid I'd get the old dear into trouble for being where I didn't belong so I hid in the crate..."

It sounded so false she knew from the look on Davy's face that he hadn't believed a word. She shrugged helplessly. "Or I could have smuggled myself on board and become trapped in that blasted crate when someone stuck another box on top."

He winked at her in that same playful way her da did and Ailish had a sudden pang. She said a silent prayer that her father was mending.

"A brave plan – not very well thought out, but a brave plan, nonetheless," Davy said casually. "So, now you're here, what do we do with you?"

Ailish's stomach flipped. Rufus Dalton had said he controlled belowdecks. Maybe this bash boy had saved her because *he* wanted to be the one to turn her over to Dalton. If Davy worked for that villain, turning in a stowaway would put him in his boss's good graces for sure. And once she was in his hands, Dalton would arrange one of his "accidents" to silence her about the golden horse.

"Heavens, will you look at the time! I'm late." Ailish edged the corners of her mouth up in what she hoped was a winning smile. "I guess I'd best be getting off now. Thanks for the warning." She inched toward the stairs again, wondering how she could get on a boat that would take her back to shore without anyone noticing. Having to leave the treasure behind galled her down to the bone, but the idea of being in Dalton's clutches was terrifying.

"I'm no friend of Mr. Dalton's," Davy said, as though he'd read her mind. "And leaving's going to be a good trick, my girl, since we're already many miles at sea."

Ailish stopped her retreat. "At sea? Impossible. I don't feel any movement."

"That's because you're aboard the *Great Eastern*. She's near seven hundred feet, longer than any wave trough, double-hulled and loaded with airtight compartments. She glides across the seas as effortlessly as an albatross rides the wind."

Ailish swallowed. "This simply cannot be. I have to get off now!" The panic in her voice was unmistakable.

"You can't," Davy assured her. "Captain Anderson isn't about to stop the cable laying for a lass like you. This is a ship of important ghost messages."

"What do you mean, *ghost messages?*"

"Why, the cable, of course! Whispers along the ocean floor for thousands of miles," he said wistfully. "Amazing. Magic, really. Those gents topside constantly send words made up of dots and dashes called Morse code back and forth, back and forth, to make sure the cable is working. I'm happy my ship is being used and wouldn't mind if this cable-laying business took a hundred years. I'm enjoying the company." He blinked as though to clear his mind. "But as for you, miss, you're going to Heart's Content with the rest of us."

Her mouth dropped open. This couldn't be happening! "Stay aboard all the way to Newfoundland – not a bit o' me!" She shook her head, still not wanting to believe it. "How will I survive?" she croaked. "I've nowhere to sleep, nothing to drink. No food! I'll starve down here!" She thought of her need to go to the toilet and averted her eyes. "And other things need attending to also..."

"Well, this is a knotty problem, isn't it? You could end up spending the entire voyage in the brig; then it's debtor's prison for you if you can't pay for your passage."

She was shocked at this prospect. "But it was an accident! I didn't mean to stay aboard. Surely, they'll let me go?"

"Captain Anderson goes by the book, sure and simple. He's not likely to give a stowaway, an *Irish* lass, no less, a free pass on his ship."

Ailish pushed the panic away, regaining control, then voiced her thoughts. "I'm stuck. We're at sea and there's no way out. That's plain enough. So, if I'm here I may as well take advantage of my predicament and go ahead with my original plan."

Her companion smiled impishly. "So you did have a plan when you got yourself locked up in that box! What was this brilliant strategy, if I might ask?"

He seemed to be enjoying her unfortunate circumstances way too much. Ailish was about to give him a blast, but then she thought of what lay ahead.

If she was going to make her way on this ship all the way to Newfoundland and find her treasure as well, it would be much easier with help, someone who knew the workings of the ship, and though she wasn't able to discern whether he was good or bad, she decided to take a leap of faith and trust Davy anyway. She would take Mr. Jones into her confidence.

"You see, I'm here to reclaim my property from Rufus Dalton."

His eyebrow arched. "Your property?"

"Yes, mine, or at least my family's. Last night, Dalton took a valuable statue of a golden horse from my da, thrashed him badly to do it too, and I'm here to get it back. I can't leave without that horse, Davy. It's our future." She hoped he'd understand how important this was.

She need not have worried. He immediately nodded, a frown creasing his brow.

"I can't abide thieving! I stay below working and try not to interfere in anyone's business, but sometimes, I must get involved and it's plain to see, this is one of those times. You have to stay aboard, alright."

"The trick's in not being discovered. There must be a way."

Davy thought about this. "You know, not so long ago, the *Great Eastern* was a luxury liner complete with cabin boys who tended to the needs of the ladies and gentlemen..."

Ailish immediately saw where this was going. "A cabin boy! Of course. The only problem being, *I'm obviously a girl.*" She planted her fists firmly on her hips and lifted her chin haughtily.

Davy looked her up and down, and then grinned wickedly. "I don't think that's a big problem. With a little decoration, we could easily hide your feminine side. I have some old clothes stored that you could wear, a disguise to hide your *obviously* being a girl and all."

The way he smirked made Ailish want to box his ears. True, she was a wee bit skinny and had no womanly curves yet, but that was no reason to mock her. She touched her waist-length hair. It was thick and framed her face in a mass of soft dark waves. Her crowning glory was the other gift she'd inherited from her ma and there was no denying it was truly feminine. "What about this?"

"Nothing to worry about, lass." Davy said appraising her coolly. "Cut it off."

Ailish stared at him in disbelief. "*Cut it off!* Are you daft?"

"It's not like an arm or a leg and the stuff will grow back."

Ailish didn't know what to say. Cut off her beautiful hair? Unthinkable! Then she thought of the little golden horse. She would have to be in disguise while she tracked down the treasure and her da had always said the best place to hide was in plain sight. Besides, she really had no choice.

Her shoulders slumped. "Where are the clothes?"

"Back there's a disused storage room where my sea locker's stowed." He indicated the rear of the hold. "Davy Jones locker, you might say. In it, you'll find most everything you need." He chuckled. "That mop of hair you'll have to deal with yourself."

"Mop, indeed!" She sniffed. "There are other problems. Where will I sleep? And don't suggest my crate! And eating – what about food?"

Davy dismissed these concerns with a wave of his hand. "Silly questions. Before it was gutted and the three cable tanks put in, this ship was designed to carry four thousand passengers and our staterooms are fit for kings and queens. There are several still held ready in case we have fancy visitors, so you could easily bunk in one of them. The rest of the crew is berthed in steerage and won't be bothering you in those fancy digs."

Davy carefully told her how to find her way through the ship to Stateroom A and to the galley to nab a bite of food.

"And as for the other things that need attending ... there are heads, *toilets*," he explained, "on each deck and a private facility in your quarters. The rest is up to you, but if it were me, I'd try to stay out of the captain's sight as long as possible."

Ailish could see this would be prudent. She may be able to fool the rest of the crew with a bit of blather, but not the captain. He'd be sure to know all those who sailed on his vessel. "I'll be invisible," she assured him.

Wending her way past a scatter of crates, Ailish went to the small storage room. In it were stacks of coiled wire rope and other ship's supplies as well as an ancient wooden locker on the floor. She opened it and there were the promised clothes. Holding them up, she saw they were dusty, but they'd fit her well enough. She tried on the striped shirt, which was only a little large, then the funny britches that, on her, tied at her ankles instead of below the knee as they had on Davy. She laughed as she pulled the green suspenders over her shoulders. The lads back home would never wear clothes like this. The styles were so old-fashioned. She guessed Davy didn't get to port often to buy new or more likely, he was like her with very few pennies to spare. This made her like him even more.

Reaching into the pocket of her trousers, she felt something hard at the bottom. Withdrawing her hand, she found an iron rivet, rusted and bent. She wondered why he would have kept such an old thing. Maybe for bash boys, it was a lucky talisman. She tucked the rivet back in her pocket.

Dealing with her hair was a problem. How would she cut it without shears?

"There's a fair to middling sharp knife in that tool box." Davy's voice from the door made her jump.

He was leaning against the door jamb, arms folded as casual as a king, watching her. Her face flushed. "How long have you been standing there?" she demanded.

"Be at ease, lass. I wasn't spying on you and your feminine self. I came to warn you that in five minutes, a work gang is coming to shift the cargo."

Ailish hurried to the box he'd indicated and, rummaging in the tools, found the knife. She picked up a hank of her silken hair and swallowed. Her da would be dreadfully disappointed – he loved her "glorious tresses" which reminded him, he said, of her ma. Then she thought of that scoundrel Dalton and the fabulous horse and her poor father lying in all that blood. She closed her eyes and sawed at the hair until it fell away. Feeling slightly sick, she picked up another handful and chopped.

Soon, her shoes were covered with her crowning glory.

Ailish returned the knife to the box and rubbed her shorn locks. She couldn't imagine what a fright she must look.

"Now you fit the part of a proper cabin boy." Davy nodded approvingly. "We'd best be going, it's late. We're well into midwatch and I know Charlie will be hankering to deal with those worn rivets in the outer hull near the bow."

"Outer hull?" she asked, stuffing her discarded clothes into the trunk to hide them from the prying eyes of any who might wander in.

"I told you my ship is double hulled." Davy went on with his chatter as they wended their way through the crates and boxes. "First of her kind in the world. She has two complete hulls, one inside the other with three feet between 'em, which makes her unsinkable, but does require twice the work from me and Charlie. I spend most of my time down there with him. He's a real tyrant."

They reached the stairs and Ailish was about to start up, when she paused to smile at her new friend. "Thanks, Davy."

"Welcome aboard the *Great Eastern*, Ailish." He gave her a jaunty salute, before sauntering off.

4

DISASTER!

.... --- .-- .-- .. -.. .-- .- ... - .... -.-..- -.... .-..

THE CLIMB TOOK AN ETERNITY, BUT THE RUMBLING
protests from Ailish's belly told her it was prudent to find
food before continuing the journey to her quarters. The
instructions Davy had given her had been from the stateroom, not belowdecks, but she was pretty sure she was
heading toward the kitchen. No, galley, she corrected herself. If she was going to pass for a salty cabin boy, she must
remember details like calling the kitchen, the galley, and
the toilet, the head.

Opening a final hatchway, Ailish suddenly found herself on the main deck, and was immediately rocked back
on her heels. She'd had no idea of the time but was still
surprised to discover it was a moonlit night with puffy
clouds silhouetted in silver. The vast bowl of the sky overhead was tranquil, but the world around her was something from a hurly-burly nightmare.

The frantic clanging of a loud gong made Ailish want
to cover her ears as she watched men scramble madly
about, some shouting orders while others ran to the

machinery that screeched and rumbled as though possessed by demons. It was mayhem.

Gawking around, she stared in awe at the gigantic ship, wondering how anything this big and made of iron could float! The deck stretched forever, covered in polished wood from a forest of trees. Six towering masts scraped the sky as five huge funnels billowed black smoke. On each side of the massive deck was a giant paddlewheel more than fifty feet across. The *Great Eastern* was truly a wonder.

Ailish took a deep breath, drawing in the fresh ocean air, then stopped. Unexpectedly, on the evening breeze she caught a faint whiff of... manure! Very strange and – she wrinkled her nose – very disgusting.

Moving forward hesitantly, she tried to orient herself and decide what to do next. Without warning, she was knocked to the ground as a heavy-set figure ran into her. Her cheek burned where it scraped on the wooden deck.

"Get out of my way, you stupid boy, before I toss you into the drink."

Ailish stared up into the shadowed face of Rufus Dalton. She hastily turned away, praying her disguise would be successful and nothing about the new look would jog her enemy's memory.

He raised his boot to give her a kick, but before he could land the blow, she was lifted out of harm's way. Someone had come onto deck behind her. As the newcomer set her down, she felt a flood of tingling warmth and goodness.

"Leave the lad alone, Dalton."

Paddy Whelan had saved her again and from his touch, Ailish was assured he was not a man to be feared.

Dalton sneered. "You have a way of vexing me that could end up very unhealthy, Whelan."

The big man shoved past Paddy and Ailish as he strode down the deck snarling orders.

"Are you alright, lad?" her rescuer asked, peering at her with concern.

"Yes, sir, thank you. What's happened?" She indicated the bedlam around them.

He gave her a funny look and Ailish wondered if he recognized her, then she dismissed the idea. The light this morning had been dim and she'd had her shawl covering her head, not to mention a skirt below. He must simply think she was thick not to know what the noise was about.

"I was in the cable tank working when the gong went off. It's a disaster, lad. We're barely eighty-two miles from Foilhummerum Bay and the cable has stopped sending. That's what the clanging is about. They ring the gong when the signal stops." He appeared puzzled by her. "You seem somewhat familiar, boy. My name is Paddy Whelan and who might you be?"

"I'm…" she thought fast. "O'Connor, sir, and I work here." She wondered if she should spit or scratch or do some other disgusting boyish thing, but found she was still too much of a young lady to try.

Paddy laughed, a rich, deep sound. "Well now,

O'Connor. There are five hundred men working on this ship and you have to be the shortest crew mate I've seen."

Ailish felt her face grow hot. "Actually, I'm a cabin boy, a *new* cabin boy and this," she indicated the madhouse around them, "is a bit overwhelming."

"Then until you get your sea legs, you'd best stay with me. Come on, lad."

Not sure if cabin boys were allowed to say no to actual sailors, Ailish obediently followed Paddy.

"Where are we going?" she asked as they dodged their way around several structures. She didn't like being out in the open inviting questions about who she was and what she was doing here.

"Past these cabooses," he pointed at the small cabins scattered about like so many squatters, before rounding a larger building and emerging onto the far side of the ship, "to the port promenade deck of the ship. Welcome to Oxford Street, O'Connor."

He motioned to the long expanse of deck and the wooden trough that ran nearly the length of the ship itself. "This is where the real work is done. You see, when we're laying the cable, it's winched out of the tanks and runs along this trough then it's carefully fed over the stern and into the ocean. It works fine until the signal stops. Then we have to raise the cable back out of the sea and repair the break. It's a perilous job. We can't put the machine in reverse to wind the cable back aboard, so it must be shackled from the yardarm and cut, then carried all the way from the stern to the bow."

"Then you fix it?" Ailish asked, curiosity getting the better of her despite worry at being discovered.

"Not quite. Once we've carried it to the bow, it's fed into a machine that dredges it to the surface and pulls it back onto the ship."

She looked out at the mirrored face of the sea reflecting the moonlight in iridescent filaments. "You drag it up from the ocean floor! How deep is that?"

"In some places, twelve thousand feet – an amazing length of cable to trail behind the ship, to be sure. The weight of it is so massive, we need a special machine just to pay it out, inch by inch."

Ailish was trying to imagine this and decided the cable must be a huge thing, as thick as a giant oak tree. She could hardly wait to see it!

It was then she noticed a small wire no wider than a man's thumb in the trough. "Hadn't you better clear that spindly stuff out before the cable is brought up?"

Again Paddy let go with his infectious laugh. "That, O'Connor, *is* the cable!"

Her eyes widened in disbelief. "What! You're joking, mister! Surely not that, that... *thread!*" Squirming past one of the men manning the wooden trough, she examined the strand more closely. It was not more than an inch across and covered in grey slimy ooze.

"That's it, alright," Paddy assured her. "And see that?" He pointed at a complicated piece of machinery. "That's the automatic release mechanism. Inside there's wheels and cogs ticking away, making sure the cable lets out just so, not too fast and not too slow. You mustn't let size fool you, lad. The automatic release is a stalwart piece of machinery, no doubt, but it's delicate as a cuckoo clock. And though the cable's little more than a wire, it be mighty as a bridge, a bridge that will span the entire ocean."

With a shouted warning to "look lively!" the sailors started the laborious task of hauling the thin cable back aboard. Instantly, everyone was hustling about the deck as they bent to their task.

"This is dangerous work, O'Connor. You can't be wandering about on your own and I've too much to do to take you to the captain. You'll have to accompany me on my watch."

So Ailish followed Paddy as he went about his tasks, her stomach feeling emptier as the minutes crawled by. Dawn came and went, then six… seven… eight o'clock.

"That's forenoon watch come and I'm done for this shift." Paddy had been working a machine called the pick-up wheel that wound the cable aboard but he now signaled another sailor to relieve him.

"What happens if the break can't be found?" Ailish asked as they leaned against the rail to watch the continuing action.

"Then, my lad, we turn tail and head back to Ireland."

Her heart skipped a beat. "Back to Ireland? We may be going home!" She thought of the last time she'd seen her da and again offered up a quick prayer that he was all right. Hope and joy sprang up in equal measure at the possibility of seeing him so soon.

"It would be a sad blow to all aboard, to be sure." Paddy sighed. "But I shan't worry about it. I'm sure we'll be able to find the problem."

"Yes, and fix it we shall!" A tall gentleman with a strong American accent interrupted as he joined them.

Ailish took note of the newcomer's deerstalker hat and Inverness cape. He was obviously not a sailor, but a proper gentleman.

Paddy nodded agreement. "Aye, that we will, sir."

"And who do we have here, Paddy?" the man asked, looking at Ailish.

"O'Connor is a cabin boy, Mr. Field." Paddy said by way of introduction. "O'Connor, this is Mr. Cyrus Field, an American gent with the vision and wherewithal to put this fantastic enterprise together."

"*Failte*, Mr. Field," Ailish said, catching herself as she was about to curtsy. That was hardly something a cabin boy would do.

"You must be the youngest crewman aboard, O'Connor." He smiled warmly. "Paddy, how much cable has come up?"

"Near as I can tell, ten miles, sir."

"That's a substantial amount to haul back aboard and we'll have to scour every inch to find that break." The tall American looked about searching for someone on the crowded deck. "I'd best confer with the other gentlemen about what to do if this rescue is unsuccessful."

"I saw Mr. Canning and Professor Thomson go into the telegraph testing caboose, sir." Paddy said helpfully.

At that moment, a shout drew everyone's attention. "Here! Come here! We've found the fault!"

Immediately, a frenzied commotion ensued around the man who had sounded the news. Ailish, Paddy and Mr. Field all hurried toward the hubbub.

When they arrived, the American pushed through the crowd to join several gentlemen who were leaning over the trough where the dead cable lay, while Paddy and Ailish hung back.

"Look at this, Cyrus," a man with a thick Scots accent indicated to Mr. Field.

"Who's the Scottish gent?" Ailish asked Paddy in a hushed tone.

"Professor Thomson, the most brilliant scientist of our time, a true genius, I heard. The other fellow is Samuel Canning; he's in charge of the actual cable laying."

Ailish watched as the three conferred. She could feel the tension in the men around her as the murmuring increased and then Mr. Field held up his hand. There was something in it. Ailish tried to get a better look, but the crowd was pressing closer and she had trouble seeing through the throng.

"Gentlemen, this is a dark day for all of us. We have but only begun our journey and here we have evidence of sabotage! This two-inch spike was driven through the cable allowing the electric current to leak into the ocean and stop the signal from reaching back to Ireland."

Ailish saw Rufus Dalton standing beside Cyrus Field. He was busy looking very important for the crowd until he caught sight of Paddy; then an evil grin appeared like a gash across his face.

"Fenians! A Fenian traitor in our midst!" he shouted to the gathered men.

Pandemonium ensued as the word spread like fire through thatch. Ailish knew that this ship was filled with English gentlemen who feared the Irish freedom brotherhood and she also realized death would be how they'd deal with anyone caught.

Mr. Field motioned for silence. "Sabotage does seem likely, Mr. Dalton, but why do you suspect the Fenians?"

"I can guarantee that wire was sound when it left the tank. I'm telling you, it's a plot. I've heard rumours the Fenians want to invade Canada and hold her ransom until the English leave Ireland. Without the telegraph cable, it would be weeks before England could answer Canada's call for help and by then, it would be too late."

Again there was a general outcry.

"Hang the traitor!"

"Throw him overboard!"

Ailish saw an imposing man in a crisp Navy uniform step forward. This, she reasoned, had to be Captain Anderson. Things were very tense and it was not the time to spring an unexpected cabin boy on him. She melted further back into the crowd.

"I will personally conduct this investigation." The captain's voice boomed over the noise, stilling the ruckus. "I want the Fenian scoundrel arrested and sent to England for treason – if we don't keelhaul him first. I will not tolerate any interference with this project."

Ailish saw Dalton look at Paddy, then draw his thumb across his throat in a gesture that made her blood run cold.

The captain called for order. "We will splice the cable and continue on our mission. Thousands of men have worked for many years to make this dream come true and we shall not be defeated. This is our chance to make history, gentlemen. Let's make that history a glorious one!"

A chorus of enthusiastic assent rose from the men and they set to work. The captain's words stirred something in Ailish, too, and she saw how, small as it seemed, the cable was bigger than any single person here. She had a feeling the transatlantic telegraph cable would change the world as she knew it.

"What happens now?" she asked Paddy, who had slid farther back into the crowd to stand beside her.

"They'll cut out the bad section and splice the end to fresh cable from the tanks. If it's still dead once we've completed this, then we have naught else to do but sail for home. We'll have done all we can."

The sun scribed its brilliant arc as it climbed ever higher in the clear blue sky but no one left Oxford Street while the splice was made. The crowd milled about, men offering help wherever needed. Paddy pulled out some sailor's hardtack and broke her off a piece. With the biscuit, Ailish was able to wait the long, tense time until at last, the cable was whole once again.

Cyrus Field left for the telegraph testing caboose to see if the freshly repaired wire would actually work. The very air around them stilled as every man and one young girl stood silently awaiting the verdict.

5

SLIP OF THE LIP

MOMENTS LATER, THE AMERICAN GENTLEMAN EMERGED from the caboose and the crowd held its breath. His face remained inscrutable but then he lifted his head and spoke the welcome words.

"The cable is working perfectly! Ireland is engaged again."

A cheer swelled from all on deck. Ailish felt her spirit leap. She was truly glad the cable was repaired and she raised her voice along with the others.

"Time to cadge a quick forty winks," Paddy said with a yawn. "Dalton's keeping an eye on me and knows when he goes off shift in two hours I'll be left on afternoon watch. I don't want the crew chief to have me up on orders for falling asleep at my post. I think you'll be safe enough on deck now that the crisis has passed. I'll see you later, O'Connor." With a wave, he left her standing amid the hustle and bustle.

Everyone else, excited at the happy news of the signal, remained to watch as the cable was returned to the sea.

Ailish herself desperately needed sleep. But first, she wanted to tell Davy what had happened. She threaded her way through the crowd, then past several cabooses to the hatch that led belowdecks. As she reached for the iron door, it flew open and Rufus Dalton stood in her path.

Ailish was so surprised, she stood rooted to the spot.

"You again! Where are you off to, boy?"

"Ah, going to get some sleep, sir." She ducked her head, not wanting to look him in the eye.

He stared down at her suspiciously. "What did you say your name was?"

Ailish gulped. "O'Connor, sir."

"Why don't I remember seeing you before today?"

"I'm not sure, sir. I'm small, maybe you overlooked me." Ailish kept her eyes downcast. For someone who was supposed to be an example to his men, Dalton was downright scruffy. His boots and wool trousers were coated in dingy black dirt, and he smelled of rank sweat.

Dalton grunted and pushed past her. "Stay out of my way, stupid boy, or I'll have you paying the devil!"

It must be another seafaring term, Ailish thought, but whatever "paying the devil" was, she knew it wouldn't be pleasant. Grateful to escape once more, she fled below to find Davy.

— - • — —

DAVY WAS IN THE HOLD WHERE AILISH HAD FIRST MET him, sitting on a large crate.

"You'll never guess what's been going on topside," she began, hoisting herself up onto the box next to him. "It's incredible." Quickly, she explained what had happened.

"At first, I wanted the cable to fail so we could go home, but now, I truly would like to see it succeed. I would be part of a great event in history, something to tell my grandchildren, that's for sure," she finished with a flourish.

"Oh, aye. To be part of this is marvellous, indeed," he agreed.

"And going home is out of the question until I solve the matter of my stolen property, anyway." Ailish thought of Dalton and his threat against Paddy. "There's something else I need to tell you, Davy, and it may take awhile."

"I'm not going anywhere and I crave a good story." He swung his legs in a most casual manner.

Wiggling in a vain attempt to get more comfortable on the hard wooden crate, Ailish explained about overhearing Dalton blackmailing Paddy for his money.

"Aye, that Mr. Dalton has been a bad one for years. Not a good soul, at all." Davy agreed. "If there's something rotten belowdecks, you can bet Dalton is behind it."

"And I haven't told you the worst part yet. He's going to make it seem like a Fenian plot is being hatched on board and Paddy is the culprit. This is why the cable fault is so frightening. It plays right into Dalton's plan and now everyone is looking for the traitor. Besides myself, Paddy is the only other Irishman aboard."

Davy shot her a teasing look.

"Irish *person* aboard," she amended. "This could go very badly for Paddy and I like him. I don't want anything terrible to happen. Now that the cable is working, I hope this tempest will blow over and the rest of the trip will be uneventful."

"And what if this friend of yours *is* a Fenian and *did* put that nail through the wire?"

Now came the tricky part. How could Ailish explain her gift without sounding as crazy as a bedbug? "I *know* Paddy didn't sabotage the cable," she began.

"Oh, and how is that?"

"I'm going to tell you something that may sound strange, even… supernatural, but it's the truth." She took a deep breath. "I can tell things about people, if they're good or evil, by touching them, or simply being near them."

Davy seemed to freeze beside her – she hoped he didn't think she was mad with her fey talk. She hurried on with her explanation. "My da calls it the second sight. That's how I know Paddy is a good man. I could feel it about him."

Several expressions crossed Davy's face at once; finally, he raised his eyebrows sceptically in a gesture Ailish knew only too well. She'd seen it on the faces of loads of unbelievers. "It's not malarkey. I can!"

"Is that so? And what does this sixth sense of yours say about me?" He crossed his arms and waited.

Closing her eyes to concentrate, she searched for the feeling that told her what the inside of someone looked like. She felt a tingle that warmed her right down to the tips of her fingers and toes. It was like nothing she'd ever had before, and it told her nothing about Davy she recognized, either good or bad. She wiggled a little closer, but still nothing.

Several tense minutes passed, then Ailish frowned. "Very odd." Tentatively, she reached out a hand for his. She had hoped it wouldn't come to this; since he didn't believe she really could see the invisible, he might get the wrong idea.

Davy shifted away and exclaimed in irritation, "Who, me? You think I'm odd!" Ailish yanked her hand back and Davy jumped down off their perch. "Thanks a lot."

"No, no, that was only a, a… slip of the lip. It's simply that, well, I don't *feel* anything from you. If I could just…" Ailish felt heat rush into her cheeks, "hold your hand to get a proper reading." She held her own hand up and wiggled her fingers.

"Oh, I see. I'm not good enough to register on your gypsy gauge."

Now she *was* irritated. "Don't be ridiculous. I'm sure if I touched you…"

"So, I'm ridiculous now!" Davy cut her off.

He was tangling her words, changing what she meant. "You don't understand," she said curtly.

"Maybe I'm too thick to figure out what a grand lady like you means!"

Storm clouds gathered in Ailish's eyes. "Stop right

there! You're putting words in my mouth."

"Am I? I'm only a simple bash boy and maybe 'simple' is the right word."

Now Ailish slid off the crate. "Simply *pigheaded*, yes!" she shot back.

"You have a strange way of treating your friends, Ailish O'Connor. I think I hear Charlie calling." He spun to leave, then stopped and turned back to her. "It's you who doesn't understand, Ails."

Ailish caught her breath at the familiar nickname.

"Anyone out here on the briny knows the ocean has many supernatural mysteries that no one can explain. And as for the cable" – his tone became superior again – "it's a long way to Newfoundland and only a fool would believe all the problems are over."

And before she could say another word, he stomped away into the darkness.

Ailish was so angry she could spit. Davy Jones was the most stubborn, obstinate, rude and unreasonable boy she had ever met! *Pigheaded* seemed a particularly accurate description.

The anger fuelled a new burst of energy and Ailish decided to go top side to find Dalton. It had been a couple of hours since Paddy had gone for his forty winks which meant a shift change was due. She'd thought about where she'd hide a valuable statue that couldn't be locked in the ship's safe, and the answer was obvious. She was sure Rufus Dalton had it stashed in his cabin. At shift change he'd be heading there for some bunk time, so this was her chance to find out where that was.

She stepped through the hatch onto the main deck and stopped in her tracks. The dreaded gong sounded once more!

6

SAFE HARBOUR

.. -. .-- ..... .- .-. .--- --- -- -.. .--- .... .- .. .-.. ... -. .-. .--.

THE CABLE HAD CEASED TO WORK AGAIN AFTER HAVING been so laboriously repaired and Ailish, exhausted herself, felt the despair of those around her as mutterings grew louder that the Fenians had struck again.

She was about to try and find Paddy to tell him what was going on, when Dalton jumped atop one of the cannons that lined the deck and called to the crowd.

"This second fault is proof of sabotage and we cannot let it go unchallenged," he shouted, stoking the unrest. "You have worked as no other crew could and I'm proud of each and every one of you. And now tired as we all are, we must splice the cable again. I haven't left this deck, but someone has and that man is our Fenian traitor. I say we find the dog and deal with him ourselves!"

There was a chorus of agreement and Ailish had to give the devil his due: Dalton had a way of speaking that was very persuasive. The men, frustrated and volatile, were close to rioting and she was sure who Dalton would suggest as a target. She couldn't believe the cable would have to be spliced again! Her own back ached at the thought. She admired the toughness of these sailors and was very glad she wasn't the one who would have to fix the blasted thing.

"Wait!" Cyrus Field pushed to the front of the throng. The American raised his hands for silence. "The signal's started again! The cable is sound once more."

A grateful murmur ran through the crowd and the relief was obvious on all the men's faces save one. Rufus Dalton looked furious and Ailish knew it was because his plot against Paddy had been foiled. With an angry curse, he jumped down from the cannon and was swallowed up by the jostling crowd.

Ailish shoved and pushed her way through the melee. She thought she caught a glimpse of him disappearing behind one of the cabooses, but when the crowd thinned and she was finally able to run after him, he was nowhere in sight.

Stumbling, Ailish decided this was too much excitement for her. She was so tired, she could hardly walk and she certainly couldn't think straight. She simply had to get some rest before tracking him to his den. That was one good thing about being at sea – no one could go far. He'd be aboard tomorrow when her brain was clearer and not muzzy from lack of sleep.

Ailish left the crowd and made her way belowdecks to find the stateroom Davy had told her about, but the ship was so immense, that before long she was thoroughly lost.

She wandered the hallways and hatchways, hopelessly muddled and feeling more dejected by the minute. She certainly wasn't going to go mincing back to Mr. Pigheaded Jones, interrupting his work to ask for directions again like some ninny.

At last, after miles of corridors and rooms and tramping from deck to deck without success, Ailish spied a sign that said Family Saloon and went to have a look, carefully closing the door behind her. Soft light from the hallway spilled in through a row of windows set high in the wall. Here was more evidence of the *Great Eastern's* earlier glory. In the room were shelves of toys and games, long disused rocking horses with real horsehair manes and tails, and children's wooden blocks with faded gold letters painted on their sides. A colourful toy box drew her like a magnet and she rummaged in it finding a china faced doll with a broken leg and a teddy bear with one eye missing as well as an entire army of lead soldiers. Tucked in a corner of the old box, a shiny brass whistle on a chain winked at her invitingly. She found it irresistible and slid it over her head, deciding no rough crewman on a cable-laying ship would want such a trifle.

It was then she noticed a divan in the corner. It looked so inviting and she was so very tired; surely it wouldn't hurt to have a small rest. Yawning, Ailish decided she would take a ten minute catnap, and then continue on. Only ten minutes…

Noises in the hallway woke her with a start. She could

hear sailors' voices and they were getting louder. She sat up when they stopped right outside the Family Saloon. Quietly, she slid off the couch and tiptoed over to the door, then pressed her ear against the cool wood. Two sailors were talking about the cable fault and the Irish Fenian traitor.

"Dalton says we can break his legs and dump him overboard when we find him." she heard one sailor say.

"It won't be the first time. Just be glad we're not on his fish food list!" the second laughed.

Ailish shuddered. What if they came into the playroom and found her? She was Irish and had no way to explain what she was doing here. What if they thought she was the Fenian and took her to Dalton?

She'd been foolish to sleep here. There was no place to hide. As she stepped back, her foot trod on a cup from a child's tea service. The fragile china shattered into a thousand pieces. The noise was a thunderclap in the silent room.

"What was that?" the first sailor asked.

"Maybe ghosties comin' for ye," the other snorted.

"Nay, man, I heard something. What's in that room?"

Ailish stared at the door knob, watching for it to turn. Holding her breath, she waited, and waited…

"You need to lay off the grog," the second ruffian growled; then, like a prayer answered, the footsteps continued and the voices faded.

She exhaled with relief. That had been too close. She

couldn't risk one more minute here. Edging the door open a crack, she checked to make sure the coast was clear, then hurriedly left the playroom feeling like a child in a game of hide and seek with Stateroom A hiding and her seeking.

Some of the corridors looked suspiciously familiar and Ailish wondered how many times she'd been down the same ones. She had no choice but to find Davy and plead with him to show her the way. She hated the idea of grovelling but had resigned herself to the upcoming humiliation when at the end of the next corridor, a sign pointed to First Class Accommodations.

Hope made her feel giddy as she hurried forward. Surely this was where she'd find her quarters. Relief quickly turned to awe as she walked toward the tall double doors marked Stateroom A. They were oak with ornate flowers and vines carved across the polished surface.

Gingerly, she twisted the handle only to have her hope sink. It held fast. She was locked out. The benefits from her nap had long since worn off and weariness weighted her eyelids again. She slumped to the floor. Now what? Looking up and down the hallway, she saw nothing she could use to help her open the door.

She noticed the small section of floor near her was scratched. It was out of place as it was the only portion of the shiny wooden hardwood that was marred in any way. She peered closer. If she scrunched her eyes just right, there appeared to be letters written in the scratches.

Silly, but she could have sworn the letters looked like

T-R-Y. Sure, she'd try, but try what? She scrutinized the solidly locked door keeping her away from her soft bed. Yes, of course, try again! The room hadn't been used in a while; maybe the door was simply stuck. She jumped up and grabbed the handle firmly twisting it but met the same stubborn resistance as before. Now breaching the door became a personal challenge. It was the same story she and every other Irishman knew too well – a fancy, rich English barrier keeping her from her heart's desire. Well, she'd see about that!

Steeling herself, Ailish backed up and launched herself at the stubborn wood, hitting it hard with her shoulder. She was sure she'd have a bruise, but it had been worth it as, with a reluctant groan, the elaborate door surrendered and swung wide.

Giving the hallway a quick check to make sure no one had heard the commotion, she stepped inside.

Her mouth dropped open as she took in the large room. The double-decked berths were draped with sumptuous curtains of red velvet and the plush chairs and couch made her want to swoon. There were gas lights in filigree sconces on the walls, a writing desk and over-stuffed chair and a rich Persian carpet on the floor. Did ordinary people actually live in splendor like this? The only person she knew who enjoyed this level of pampering was Uncle Peter, and he was a knight with a castle! Perhaps this had been the accommodation of kings and queens.

She unlaced her boots, quickly kicking them off, and then squished her toes in the thick carpet, sighing with pleasure. A reflection in the large gilded mirror caught her eye and she stopped. Who was that scarecrow looking back?

Her chopped auburn hair stuck out at all angles and her sunken cheekbones made her cornflower blue eyes look enormous. With her shabby clothes and dirty face, she looked like an urchin from the backstreets of Dublin.

Moving to the washstand, Ailish was delighted to see fresh water in the pitcher. Piling her clothes on the beautiful couch, she poured a generous splash into the delicate porcelain bowl and cleaned up as best she could. With trembling fingers, she clambered into the snug, soft bed and lay back with a sigh. The cotton sheets were crisp and the feather counterpane was as light as... well, as a feather! She thought of her da and sent him a good-night kiss. Drifting off, she couldn't help but feel she'd found a safe harbour here in her luxury digs and that, there was no denying, she owed to Mr. Davy Jones.

7

DIRTY BUSINESS

THE NEXT MORNING, AILISH AWOKE STARVING. EVEN A good old potato fry-up would be a treat. It was odd how, not having it, one could miss and desire the very thing one had tried to escape. Stretching, she looked around the wonderful room, half expecting it to be a dream, but was pleased to find herself still surrounded by the riches she'd found the night before. She kicked off the sumptuous comforter and prepared to start her day. Food was top of her list, followed closely by tracking and spying on Dalton.

Ailish washed and dressed in a hurry, then set out for the galley. Davy's directions floated in her head, but nothing made sense when she tried to apply it to the actual layout of the ship. She poked about for a while, afraid of repeating yesterday's disastrous route march, then decided to follow the herd and tucked into line behind a group of fine-looking gentlemen who were chatting about what they would have for breakfast.

In the spacious dining room, Ailish was again

astounded by the grandness of the *Great Eastern*. The white linen cloths on the tables accented the fine china and crystal glasses, large oil paintings adorned the walls and brocade upholstery covered the chairs.

As she watched, a waiter took a gentleman's order and disappeared into what had to be the galley. Ailish followed at a discreet distance. She slid into the room behind the waiter and felt her mouth water with the delicious smells that greeted her. She would stock up with as much food as possible before making her escape.

On a cooling rack, a large stack of fragrant fresh-from-the-oven buns sat waiting in a basket. The delicious smell was so enticing, it made her dizzy. She crouched below the countertop, then carefully reached up and felt around blindly searching for the tasty morsels.

"Ouch!" A stinging slap made her draw her hand back.

"What do you think you're doing?"

A giant of a man with a large bushy moustache towered over her, brandishing a long soup ladle like a sceptre.

"I'm the new cabin boy," she faltered, "and I was looking for a bite of food. You have so much here; I didn't think you'd miss a bit." She edged backward toward the door. "I'm sorry to have bothered you, sir."

The rotund man laughed heartily. "I don't care who you are and there's no need to steal food aboard this ship. There's plenty for all."

He tossed her one of the warm buns and Ailish

stopped her retreat. *Plenty* was not a word she'd ever associated with food – meagre, sparse, scarce, yes, but never plenty.

As she ravenously devoured the best bread roll in the history of the world, the cook began piling all manner of good things onto a large plate. "On deck, we have a cattle pen with ten bullocks, one milk cow, one hundred and fourteen sheep, twenty pigs, twenty nine geese, fourteen turkeys and five hundred other fowl! We certainly have food enough to feed a shipwrecked waif like you."

Ailish's stomach let out a loud rumble of appreciation and the cook roared with laughter again. The animal smell she'd sniffed when she'd first gone on deck was now explained. The variety of creatures on board sounded like the passenger list from Noah's Ark!

He passed her the mile-high mountain of savoury food. "You come back here any time you're feeling peckish between meals and Henry will fix you up fine." He twirled and spun the ladle in a display as elaborate as any performed by a drum major. "But in future, Henry thinks you should eat your meals in the crew's mess. The gentlemen you find in this salon" – he motioned to the grand dining hall with the ladle – "they like to *talk* about work, and that's about all they have to do with it. With the crew, you'll find a class of men who not only know the value of hard work, but can ably perform those duties and you are sure to enjoy their company more."

Henry the cook told her where the crew took their

meals, then turned back to his army of assistants while Ailish wondered how long it would take her to eat the generous feast.

She made her way to the crew's mess where she found a hidden corner, away from the boisterous men, to enjoy her bounty in peace. There was no way she could finish the enormous plateful, but she tried her best. As she sat back stuffed and well contented, her stomach rolled and a loud belch erupted from her belly, making her face flush with embarrassment. She glanced around to see if anyone had heard her and saw Rufus Dalton leaving the mess. She'd been so busy gobbling her food that she hadn't noticed him come in.

Ailish dusted the crumbs from her hands. No matter – it was perfect timing; she was finished and he was on his way out. Depositing her dishes in a kitchen trolley, she left to follow her prey.

Once on deck, Ailish hid behind a caboose to watch Dalton as he went about ordering his men to the various tasks involved in laying the cable, fixing machinery and running the ship.

After a couple of hours, she began to lose hope that he would do anything but normal boring work. At this rate, finding the horse would take much longer than she had thought.

Around mid-morning, Dalton walked over to one of the crew. "I'm going to take an early dinner. I'll be back in an hour."

Ailish was still full as a tick from her enormous breakfast, but she wasn't about to let Dalton out of her sight now and stealthily followed him belowdecks.

She was surprised when, instead of going to the crew's mess, he took a set of stairs she'd never seen before. They passed no sailors as they descended into the deepest regions of the giant ship. She'd never been this far down into the belly of the *Great Eastern*. The noise of the engines grew louder and the light became poorer the further they went.

Being careful to stay a safe distance behind, she watched as Dalton spun a large wheel on an iron hatchway marked Boiler Room. She waited until he'd entered and closed the heavy door then dashed to follow, praying the hatch wasn't too massive for her to manoeuver. Struggling, Ailish managed to pry the door open wide enough to slip through, then with a gigantic effort, pulled it shut and spun the wheel. She didn't like the idea of sealing herself in with Dalton, but neither did she want to be discovered because she was careless and left a door open.

The world that greeted her was one conjured from a nightmare. Surrounding her were eight gigantic boilers that groaned and moaned, hissing like restless dragons. Eerie red fingers of light came from huge furnaces into which men ceaselessly shovelled large piles of coal and beyond, a mass of machinery clanged and howled. The noise was deafening and the heat suffocating.

Ahead of her she could see more coal, mountains of it! Everywhere she looked, there was coal. She remembered when she'd first met Dalton that fateful night back in Foilhummerum Bay, he'd boasted the *Great Eastern* carried fifteen thousand tons of coal, enough to sail nearly around the world. At the time she'd thought it impossible; now she believed every word.

Dalton was nowhere to be seen. She walked up to a dust-blackened sailor; sweat gleamed on his shirtless back as he toiled with a shovel. "Excuse me, have you seen Mr. Dalton?"

The man pointed toward a black opening in the wall. "That's the tunnel that runs through the coal bunkers. He went in there."

Once inside the metal channel, she shivered. Compared to the boiler room, it felt cold and was very dark. The only light was that which seeped in from either end of the long shaft. The sound of footfalls made her stop. Far ahead, someone was moving down the tunnel. The silhouette of the figure grew clearer as he neared the far end and the light brightened. It was Dalton, but what was he doing down here? Was this another part of his duties?

She started after him. Everywhere the thick coal dust swirled and eddied like Satan's breath. It filled her lungs and the choking sensation made her want to gasp and fight for air.

He'd nearly reached the end of the tunnel when Ailish felt a cough start deep in her chest. She tried to stifle the noise, but she was drowning in dust and her breath exploded out of her in a wracking spasm.

Dalton immediately stopped and turned. "Who's there?"

She plastered herself to the wall not wanting to be framed in the light behind her.

"Ails, back here! Hurry!"

She whirled. It was Davy's voice. He must have gotten over their tiff and his timing couldn't have been better. Scrambling, she'd almost reached the safety of her side of the tunnel when a shouted command boomed out behind her.

"You there, halt! I said stop where you are!"

"May the saints preserve us!" Ailish prayed silently. Dalton was coming back after her.

She sped out of the iron hallway expecting to find Davy, but he was nowhere to be seen. He must have gone on ahead to open the hatchway. She raced forward, her breath coming in small gasps, but stopped in surprise when she reached the metal door. It was shut tight. Why had Davy closed the darn thing before she'd made it out?

Cursing, she struggled with the heavy iron portal as precious seconds flashed by. With a groan, she shoved hard on the stubborn hatch which finally opened a fraction.

She wiggled through to find Davy waiting on the far side. "Why did you close the door?" she asked, irritated.

"It swung shut behind me!" he protested.

"Well, help me close the wretched thing again!" she

wheezed. Together they leaned against it, but even with Davy's shoulder helping, it took every ounce of her strength to move the massive hatch. How could it have swung shut? Ailish suspected Davy had panicked and closed the door in fear, but his pride wouldn't let him admit to that. The coal dust on the floor caused her shoes to slip and she fell, grazing her head. She struggled to her feet and began again. At last, it sealed itself with a resounding clang.

"Someone should oil this thing!' she muttered as she spun the big locking wheel. "We have to find a wedge so Dalton can't turn it from the other side." Darting her eyes around the deserted hallway, she saw nothing that would help.

"There's no time!" Davy warned. "You head topside and I'll try to slow him down. He can't do anything to you in front of the crew and besides, it was dark back there. I'm sure Dalton didn't see it was you."

If this was Davy's way of making up for the panic attack at the door, it was foolishly dangerous. "If you're caught, he'll beat the daylights out of you. Come with me," she pleaded.

"I'll be safe, Ails. Charlie's going to meet me here any second and Dalton's no match for my boss. We'll stall him as long as we can. Trust me." He smiled at her then pointed to the stairway.

Ailish saw this was her only chance and there was no time for arguing. She ran for the stairs that led to the higher decks. Davy was right, it had been dark in the passage and she was sure Dalton didn't get a good look, but she couldn't let him catch her. He was no fool and he'd know it was her following him and that would be the end of the search and maybe her also. She started up, trying to move quickly, but her shaking legs didn't want to obey.

The boom of the hatch being thrown open below reverberated up the iron stairway. Davy and Charlie wouldn't be able to distract him for long and Dalton would be coming after her any second. The ruffian might not have seen who it was in the dim tunnel, but if he made it to the stairway and saw her climbing, he'd recognize her for sure. She quickened her pace.

Emerging onto the next deck up, Ailish saw that the stairway emptied onto a corridor that extended left and right. Which way should she go? In her mind, she tossed a coin. Left it was! She ran for the far end and, she prayed, the stairs to the next deck.

Disappearing would be good, but no handy hidey-hole presented itself. Ahead, at the base of the stairwell, was a small alcove with a wooden desk. Strewn across the surface, she saw a discarded tea mug and a tobacco pouch beside a pipe. The ivory pipe bowl was beautifully decorated with ornate scrimshaw. On the floor beside the desk was a metal wastebasket filled with balls of discarded paper.

An idea hit her. She couldn't hide, but she could create one devil of a distraction.

Ailish moved to the desk and picked up the pouch.

Inside, she found what she was looking for – the wooden matches that went along with the pipe and tobacco.

Perfect! She struck one and it flared to life. Holding it to a corner of one of the balls of paper, she was rewarded with a puff of smoke, and then a brilliant orange flame as the edge caught. She dropped the burning paper into the basket.

A second match soon had another piece aflame. The smoke was rolling out of the wastebasket now. Ailish left the crackling fire and fled to the stairs.

Through the billows of smoke boiling out of the alcove, Ailish saw Dalton clamber up from the lower deck. Everyone knew the worst thing a seaman could imagine was a fire aboard ship and even though he was a ruffian and a bully, Rufus Dalton was also a serious sailor and he would stop to put out the small blaze before coming after her.

The last thing Ailish saw as she pulled the stairway door closed behind her was Dalton kicking over the basket and stomping on the flames with his big dirty boots.

The small fire wouldn't stop him for long and when she stepped into the bright sunlight topside, she immediately looked around for someplace to blend in.

It was then Ailish looked down and saw she was covered with coal dust. If Dalton saw that, it wouldn't matter that he hadn't caught her, he'd know it had been her following him. The sound of plaintive bleating made her turn her head toward the far end of the deck. There she saw her salvation.

Running, she grabbed a shovel and bucket and climbed into the large pen that held the herd of sheep. She hesitated a moment, not believing what she was about to do, then threw herself down into the smelly straw and rolled around. Jumping up, Ailish began calmly shovelling the animal dung into the bucket.

At that moment, Dalton charged onto the deck and his gaze swept the scene. He stalked toward the sheep pen and Ailish felt her breath stop in her chest.

Had he recognized her as the phantom from below?

Head down, she continued shovelling as he scrutinized her. She could feel his eyes burning into her and tried to look as innocent as if she'd been at church all this time and not fleeing for her life belowdecks.

"You been here all shift, boy?" he asked suspiciously.

"As you can see, I'm cleaning up after the sheep, sir." She scooped up a steaming shovel full of dung and tossed it toward the bucket. Her aim wasn't the best and some of the greasy muck splashed onto Dalton's shoes, landing with a stinking plop.

"You stupid boy! Look what you've done." He shook off the pungent mess.

Ailish smiled; then despite a valiant effort to stopper it, a giggle escaped, dragging a laugh with it. She couldn't help it. Yes, she was quite the young lady standing there up to her knees in sheep dung and covered in smelly straw. Her da would be so proud!

Dalton didn't see the humour and his face went beet red with rage. "You think that's funny, boy..." He grabbed for her.

Hastily backing away, Ailish skidded in something slimy and fell into the muck. The laughter was now past her control and she hoped nothing would accidentally fly into her open mouth as she thrashed around trying to stand again.

"The sights you don't see, *and smell,* when out for a brisk walk on deck!" Paddy Whelan stood with an amused look on his face, watching the pantomime.

"This bilge rat is going to wish he'd never been born!" Dalton pushed his sleeves up as he prepared to beat Ailish.

"Relax, Dalton, the lad's the one needing to walk the plank to wash away all that mess. I'd say you and your boot got off lightly."

A crewman called Dalton's name and indicated he needed some help with a piece of machinery.

The brutish crew chief glared at Ailish. "I'll get you for this. You'll be lucky if you don't wake up in forty fathoms of seawater." He stomped away cursing with some colourful language Ailish had never heard before.

That had been too close. She clambered out of the byre, brushing as much of the stinky straw as possible off her clothes. A ewe eyed her dubiously, baa-ing her disapproval. Ailish reached back over the railing and patted the animal. "Thanks, old girl." The ewe must be ready for shearing as she was as round as a stuffed sausage.

"And thank you, Paddy. I owe you again." Ailish shook a green gooey mystery gob off her finger.

Paddy grimaced. "You'd best not let the captain find you like that, O'Connor. He'd have you in the brig for assaulting an officer's nose!"

Ailish winced as she caught a whiff of herself. "Ach, you're right about that. Since the damage is done, I'll finish my shift cleaning the pens, and then I'll have a go at myself."

"You may want to do us all a favour and have your meals delivered out here!"

Ailish grinned as she climbed back into the pen.

Paddy must have thought her truly unfit for human company, because one of the galley crew did deliver her food at the end of the watch – which by then she gratefully accepted, sitting with the fat ewe to eat.

When it came time to go below and wash, she had no idea how she would accomplish this task. She had a little water left in the jug in her room, but doubted it would be enough to remove the ground-in residue left over after she had scraped the worst off with the straw. And there would still remain the problem of her clothes. She had only what she was wearing and scrubbing them was going to be tough.

She made it to the safety of her cabin, still wondering what to do about her pungent problem. Once inside the sumptuous state room, she immediately saw a note stuck to the ornate settee. "OPEN ME!"

It must be from Davy, but what did it mean? She stripped off her soiled breeches and sat down on the couch to re-read the odd note again. "OPEN ME!" Who was *me?* She looked down at where she was sitting. It was a very beautiful couch...

Springing to her feet, Ailish pulled up on the seat cushion. It gave on smooth hinges, revealing a large tub hidden beneath. The bath was filled with steaming water and fragrant bubbles. "Thank you, thank you, *thank you!*" she laughed. Bless Davy for giving her this fabulous surprise. His timing was perfect – again.

As she pulled off the rest of her filthy clothes, she noticed a wooden washboard leaning against the end of the tub. Of course. She'd scrub herself first, then her clothes in the same water. They would dry by morning and when next she hunted Rufus Dalton, she'd be as fresh as a daisy.

She eased down into the bath, relishing the soothing effect of the hot water. Her head was tender where she'd hit it and her muscles ached from wrestling with the massive door, not to mention the hours of mucking out the animal enclosures.

Grabbing a fistful of the abundant soap suds, she inhaled the lilac scent, leaving a unicorn horn of white froth on her nose. She clapped her hands, squirting bubbles through her fingers then piled more of the fragrant foam on top of her hair in spiralling devil's horns.

How had Davy done this magic? She paused. Davy...

Ailish dove beneath the water, and then peeked over the edge of the tub. "David Jones, you're not lurking around in here, are you?" she asked the empty room. Silence was her only reply.

Relieved she was truly alone, she relaxed and lay back in the deep tub thinking of how to find the wonderful horse. Today's efforts had almost turned into a disaster. She reminded herself to thank Davy for the help in the tunnel and for the much needed bath. As for her prize, she would have to switch tactics to find it.

8

DISCOVERED!

WHEN AILISH WENT BELOW THE NEXT MORNING, SHE found Davy sitting on his favourite crate. "Ahoy!" she began in an effort to be more cabin-boyish. "Thank you for all the help yesterday. It was close. How did you get away from that goon, anyway? I didn't see any way out but up those stairs. Oh, and, thanks for the bath. It was perfect." She stopped, feeling embarrassed at her non-stop palaver. The warm tingle she had felt before had returned.

His face broke into an amazing smile. "It was very entertaining."

Ailish had a moment of panic, thinking of her bubble escapades. "You mean the chase through the ship, right?"

"Of course, lass. It's not often I can be part of a dash like that."

"Why didn't you find me after Dalton left?" she asked, remembering how he had disappeared.

"Oh, the lads above decks don't want to see the likes of me and Charlie. We're not their sort and we don't much like to fraternize with those riff-raff sailors either. Our place is below and we generally stay there. We like it in the belly of our ship." He winked at her. "Besides, someone had to arrange your much needed surprise."

"But after all that, I'm no closer to finding the golden statue. I'm sure Dalton brought it aboard and I think I know where he's hidden it. All I need is a genie from a lamp to tell me where his cabin is." She sighed in her most pitiful way and leaned against the crate next to Davy, trying to look demure. She needed to find that cabin and if anyone knew where it was, it would be David Jones, bash boy.

"I'm not a genie, exactly, but I know where Dalton's cabin is. Never been in it of course, that's against my principles to snoop in a man's home, but I can tell you where to find it."

Ailish brightened. This was exactly what she'd hoped he'd say. "Really? Well, I don't have any such scruples. The man's a thief and I intend to take my property back." She held out a pencil she'd found in her cabin and the piece of paper with OPEN ME! written on it. "You can draw the directions on the clean side of this. I sort of, well to tell the truth, I have a little trouble remembering all those *turn-lefts-and go-rights* you give me. It's so confusing belowdecks."

Davy shook his head as though she was the class

dunce and Ailish opened her mouth to protest when he pointed at a folded sheet of worn paper on the crate next to him. "I thought you might want to know where the scurvy dog holed up, so I already drew you a map."

She abandoned the old note and reached for the tattered paper. On it was a neat diagram showing the interior of the ship and a complicated path from Stateroom A to Dalton's cabin on one of the lower decks. She tucked the map into her pocket. "Perfect! Thanks for this and thank you again for the magic bath. I've never been pampered like that."

"I couldn't have you running around my ship smelling like a barnyard, now, could I?" He laughed then peered off into some dark recess. "I think I hear Charlie calling. The man's a slave driver. See ya." He ambled away whistling a sea shanty.

She watched him go and the warm feeling faded. Davy was a strange boy, but she liked him.

Rufus Dalton, however, was another matter. Yesterday had surely solidified his hatred of her and it might not be a bad thing to enlist some stronger help. Breakfast was a good place to do this.

As she jumped off the crate, Ailish picked up the OPEN ME note and glimpsed at it. She must have splashed water on it during her fabulous bath for the ink had blurred and washed away. Thinking of those iridescent bubbles made her smile all over again. She would enjoy reliving this luxury when she and her da were once again trundling all over Ireland in their caravan – that is, if she didn't find her horse.

— - • — —

When Ailish entered the crew's mess, she spotted Paddy sitting at a table finishing his meal. He was in the middle of the room, and no way did she want to talk to him out there in the open in case the captain strolled in.

She waved from behind a wide support column, but he didn't notice her. With no other choice, she stealthily nabbed one of Henry's delicious buns off the plate of a passing sailor, then took a quick bite before hurling it at Paddy. She hated to waste one of the delicacies, but it was for a good cause. He straightened.

"Come here!" She gestured frantically.

He looked confused, then got up and followed her behind the pillar.

"What on earth are you up to, boy?" He sniffed, then smiled. "You certainly look and smell better than the last time I laid eyes on ye."

Ailish made a face at him, then relented. "Thank you again for helping." Hesitantly, she cleared her throat. "Er, Paddy... I wanted to warn you about Dalton. I think he's a dangerous man and you should be careful."

His face first showed surprise, then suspicion. "And why would you say that, lad?"

She took a deep breath and plunged on. "I was in the hold when Dalton threatened to expose you as a Fenian if you didn't give him your money and I heard two of his gang say they had his permission to throw the traitor overboard, after they broke his legs! I know he's out to get you."

Paddy's surprise turned to shock at her abundant knowledge and he seemed about to protest, then instead, slowly nodded his head. "You are a wonder, lad, and aye, Dalton's threat is real, but I can take care of myself. Besides, from what I've seen, I'd say he's out to get the both of us." He tousled her roughly cropped hair. "I'll tell you what. You watch my back and I'll watch yours, that way, the scoundrel can't sneak up on either of us."

Ailish liked this idea and knew the time was right to tell Paddy about the stolen horse. Perhaps with their new friendship, he could help her. "Agreed, but there's something else I have to tell you about Rufus Dalton and why I'm on this ship."

Before she could say another word, Captain Anderson entered the room.

Ailish's eyes widened. "Oh, Jesus, Mary and Joseph! I've got to go. I'll talk to you later." And with that, she disappeared out a rear door to the mess, leaving Paddy scratching his head at her odd behaviour.

— - • — —

READING THE MAP, AILISH FOLLOWED THE TWISTS AND turns marked on the paper as she made her way to Dalton's cabin. At last, she was only a couple of corridors away. Her golden treasure was practically in her hands. Holding the paper out in front of her, she checked she was heading in the right direction.

As she rounded the corner, she collided with Cyrus Field, his deerstalker cap and cape fluttering out behind him.

"Oh, beg pardon, sir!" Hastily, she folded the map so he wouldn't see the penciled-in trail that led to Dalton's cabin, which Davy had marked with a convenient X.

"Well, hello, my young friend. What are you up to this morning? Secret letters to be delivered?" He indicated the folded paper.

Ailish didn't know what to say. She remembered the last time she'd seen the grand gentleman. He'd rushed into the crowd with news that the cable was working and thus had foiled Dalton's plan to make Paddy give him his money. "Ah, no sir. I'm on my way to the, the… telegraph message cabin. Yes, I have a very important message for the message cabin. No time to chat, Mr. Field." She made to move past him.

"If you mean the telegraph testing caboose, then I can save you a lot of time. You're heading in the wrong direction to get topside. The stairs are that way." He pointed over her shoulder. "You know, O'Connor, I believe I'll go and check in on the communications with Ireland myself. Come along, boy, I'll show you a shortcut."

Ailish gave him a strained smile. She was cornered. Obediently, she joined the American as she tried to figure a way out of this predicament. Parading on the main deck with a notable like Cyrus Field could only lead to discovery and disaster.

"I hope you have that message memorized, O'Connor," Mr. Field said as they marched briskly on.

"Why, sir?"

"Because once inside the caboose you won't be able to read it," the learned gentleman explained. "The telegraph operators need total darkness to monitor the strength of the electric signal running through the cable. They measure a small pinpoint of light that is thrown onto a special gauge called a galvanometer. If the light jumps off that gauge, we have a fault and the signal stops. No telegraph messages can get through. It's then that one of the men springs outside the caboose and rings that blasted gong."

"My friend Davy calls them ghost messages, whispering across the ocean floor," said Ailish.

Mr. Field smiled down at her. "What a whimsical idea. Who is this Davy?"

"He's the boy in the hold, about my age and he knows ever so much about this ship."

Mr. Field opened the last hatchway. "I haven't met this Davy. He must be new, like you – or perhaps it's the vast size of this ship and the huge crew we took on in England. Sometimes, I feel like I'll never have all the passageways memorized."

Ailish laughed. "Davy is not a new crewman. From the way he talks, you'd think he built this old boat. He works a lot and says he likes it belowdecks better." They stepped into the bright sunshine on the busy deck and Ailish knew how Davy felt. She would rather have been safe below and not exposed up here where everyone could see her. Furtively, she glanced around, praying the captain was busy elsewhere. She didn't want to explain who she was or what she was doing on his ship. That would win her a one way ticket to the brig. She trailed behind Mr. Field and decided once they got to the testing caboose, she'd make up some excuse to leave, then go back to find Dalton's cabin. She'd been so close.

But when they arrived at the caboose, Mr. Field insisted she go through the curtained door first. Immediately, they were plunged into total darkness. Actually, she decided, inside a dark room was a good place to hide. She could sit quietly in a corner and no one would know she was there.

"O'Connor, where are you, boy? Give your message to the operators so they can send it." Cyrus Field's disembodied voice commanded from out of the darkness.

Oh, dear. She'd forgotten about that. She couldn't think of an excuse to exit gracefully and she certainly wasn't about to give over her map. She had to get out of there now!

Turning, she blundered blindly toward what she hoped was the door and slammed smack into a body just entering the darkened room. The force of her impact sent them both sprawling onto the deck.

"By thunder! Who are you and what are you doing on my ship?" an angry voice bellowed.

Ailish scrambled to her feet. In an undignified heap in front of her was a red-faced man in a fancy naval uniform with lots of gold buttons.

She had bowled over Captain Anderson, master of the *Great Eastern,* and behind him stood Rufus Dalton!

9

TRAPPED!

AILISH WAS NOW IN A SECTION OF THE SHIP SHE WOULD rather have avoided – the captain's office.

"Name?" Captain Anderson asked tersely. He held a black fountain pen poised over an official-looking form that was laid out on his desk.

"O'Connor, sir," Ailish replied timidly, visions of a damp and dingy cell filling her head.

The captain proceeded to write this down. "I shall require your first name as well and the port where you stowed away on my ship."

She was stumped now. Ailish was an Irish girl's name and it would be a dead giveaway to Rufus Dalton, who had accompanied them to the office and continued to stare at her through his hooded reptilian eyes, as though trying to place her.

"Ah, Liam, sir, Liam O'Connor. And I boarded your ship in…" She couldn't say Foilhummerum Bay in case it twigged Dalton's memory. She tried to think of the last stop the *Great Eastern* had made before setting off for

Ireland. She'd heard scuttlebutt that the cable had been brought on board somewhere in England. Shropshire? Shornette? "Sheerness, Captain! Sheerness, back in England."

Both the captain and Dalton looked at her in surprise.

Dalton shook his head in disbelief. "But the brat's Irish, sir, don't seem right he'd be from England."

The captain's glare softened. "Since the Great Potato Famine, life has not been easy in Ireland, Mr. Dalton. Perhaps this boy's family emigrated to England." Then his tone became a fraction gentler. "And our young stowaway then decided he would rather be in Newfoundland."

"That's right, sir." Ailish eagerly agreed, knowing sympathy when she heard it. "I have relatives in Heart's Content who I'm going to stay with and I figured since you were going there, I'd hitch a ride." That part of the story, anyway, was somewhat true.

Dalton scoffed derisively. "I saw him with Paddy Whelan. They're thick as thieves those two, sir."

"Mr. Whelan helped me a couple of times, yes, that's true, but he doesn't know I'm a stowaway. He thinks I'm a cabin boy." Ailish defended Paddy, knowing Dalton was looking for any excuse to show her friend in a poor light.

"That's neither here nor there," Captain Anderson interrupted. "My concern now is what to do with you for the duration of the voyage. I'm not prepared to throw you in the brig, although you will be turned over to the authorities when we get to port. Since you're impersonating a cabin boy, you can indeed assume the duties of one: running messages, feeding livestock and the like. God knows Henry could use some help with that zoo he brought on board."

Ailish saw a tiny opportunity to make things better without actually lying to the captain. "Yes, sir, I was cleaning the sheep pen yesterday." True enough, when the wind was right, she could still detect a faint whiff of dung from her clothes.

"Without being told?" Captain Anderson nodded approvingly. "That's the initiative I'm looking for. Continue to make yourself useful. If you're man enough to be aboard the *Great Eastern,* then I expect you to take your duties seriously. Mr. Dalton will oversee you and assign tasks so that you contribute to this ship. You will report to him and remember, Mr. O'Connor, he will report to me. Have I made myself clear?"

"Aye, aye, Captain!" Relief flowed over her like a cool breeze. Now that she was out in the open, she would have more opportunity to snoop. This unfortunate run in had turned out better than she could have wished for.

Dalton's huge paw clamped her arm and she winced. "Come with me, boy." He yanked her out of the captain's office and shoved her hard against the wall. "I don't know what you're up to, but I'm keeping an eye on your every move. Your skinny Irish bones belong to me for the rest of the trip and the first order of business is this – you stay away from your pal Whelan, got it? He's no longer going to save you from having your ears boxed whenever I feel like a little exercise. If you so much as spit on the deck, I'll see you spend the rest of this voyage in the bottom of the bilge as food for the rats. Now get a brush and start sweeping!" He shoved her roughly away from him.

Ailish shivered. She hated rats. Nodding mutely, she slid past the angry crew chief and went to find a broom.

— - • — —

TRUE TO HIS WORD, FOR THE NEXT SEVERAL DAYS DALTON kept her so busy, Ailish was exhausted by nightfall. Some of the other members of the crew noticed the way she was being worked and looked sympathetic, but none seemed willing to challenge Dalton's authority. She had no choice but to be a good cabin boy and run errands, scrub and paint anything that stood still, sweep the deck and tend to the animals. She had never worked so hard in her life.

Ailish kept the image of her da in her head and tried to be very patient. It would be worth it in the end and the bully couldn't keep on hounding her forever. She just had to outlast him.

It took a long, painful while, but once Dalton seemed assured that she was of no further importance, he did exactly what she thought he'd do – he relaxed his guard. The day came when she knew it was time to begin the hunt once more. She kept the map Davy had drawn tucked in her pocket, always waiting for her chance to slip away and make it down to the third-class quarters where the crew slept.

The afternoon air had grown very still and the sky had an ominous green cast. A squall was coming and from the way the crew was preparing, Ailish suspected it would be a fierce one. As she watched, Dalton shouted orders to secure lifeboats and tie down loose equipment in preparation for the stormy weather to come. He was a harsh taskmaster, but he knew his job and the men jumped to it when he roared his orders.

As the big man strode up and down the long teak deck like an army general gone berserk, Ailish calmly continued to put out hay and oats, clean old straw and tend to the chickens, all the while surreptitiously keeping an eye on her jailor, waiting for her moment.

Finishing the day's egg collection, she ducked out the low door of the wooden chicken coop to find Paddy leaning against its side, his arms crossed over his chest.

"The word is going about that we have a stowaway aboard." He raised his eyebrows at her in a questioning way and Ailish felt her stomach sink. "This villain is purported to be about your height and also your age, with close cropped dark hair." He scrutinised her short locks before going on. "And dressed, well, dressed exactly like you. This ruffian was discovered when he met Captain Anderson in a most impolite manner. Now, with us being such good mates and all..." Here he paused and Ailish felt the weight of the lie she'd told to him. "I'm sure we'd confide in each other if we knew anything. You wouldn't be able to shed any light on this mystery rogue, would you, lad?"

Ailish's spirit plummeted. She had few friends on board, two to be precise, and now she'd been caught being false to one of them.

"I can explain, Paddy. I lied to you and for that, I'm truly sorry, but I had to stay." She looked down at the eggs while she gave him the halfpence account of the incident, absently rubbing the wicker basket's edge with her finger. When she was finished, she snuck a look up at his face.

He didn't look much better. "Let me get this straight. You knock the captain down, in front of his men, then tell him you stowed away on his ship while it's on the most important voyage in history. You're lucky Captain Anderson didn't string you up from the yardarm!"

She noticed the merry twinkle in his eyes was back and saw how he was trying not to smile. She'd been forgiven and they both knew it. The sinking feeling evaporated and the sun seemed to shine a little brighter.

"But the worst thing that came out of it is that Rufus Dalton is now in charge of me and he's a beast. He says I can't go near you or he'll throw me in the bilge to be eaten by rats!"

"Nonsense," Paddy scoffed.

"You don't know what that monster is capable of!" A vision of her father's bloody face swam in front of her eyes and she shuddered. "Maybe he will!"

"I told you we're mates. I'll keep a weather eye out for

you, lad. Dalton's a bully who likes scaring those he can." He gestured to the hen house. "And it appears you've been a little chicken when dealing with our crew chief. You must like smelling foul."

Ailish plucked a stray feather out of her hair and waved it under her nose. "Smelling fowl, no, but they do provide a smashing breakfast." She brandished the basket of newly gathered eggs.

Laughing, Ailish noticed Dalton looking their way. She immediately dropped the feather and pulled the basket closer to her. "I'm not supposed to talk to you."

Paddy followed her gaze, then scowled. "I wouldn't let that blowhard tell you what to do."

"But I have to. He's my new boss, or maybe warden is a better word. I can't get into any more trouble or it could spoil my plan."

Her agitation must have showed as Paddy's tone changed immediately. "There's more to this than you're saying, O'Connor. Perhaps you'd better tell me everything."

"I will, but not here." Ailish checked to see if Dalton was coming their way. "Later, I'll meet you in the machinery storage hold. I'll ask Davy to join us and we'll explain what's been going on."

"Davy? Who is this Davy? Another stowaway?" Paddy asked.

"He's the bash boy who works belowdecks." When Paddy still looked confused she went on. "He helps

Charlie the riveter keep the ship's iron plates in good order..."

Paddy was about to say something when a shout stopped them both.

"Get back to work O'Connor, before I have you scrubbing Oxford Street with a holystone!" Rufus Dalton bellowed from high on the narrow catwalk that spanned the deck from one giant paddlewheel housing to the other.

"I'm done work after the second dogwatch. Meet me below then."

From what Ailish had been able to pick up from the sailors she'd overheard, the language of the sea was complicated and it occurred to her that she may have told him the wrong time. "That's eight o'clock tonight, right?"

He laughed. "Yes it is, right after first dogwatch, which is when you should be having your supper, and before evening watch when you should be sleeping. It's a good thing you aren't a real cabin boy, O'Connor. You'd miss your meals!" He was still chuckling as he strode off down the deck.

Ailish went to the sheep enclosure and checked the stable for Dimples, which is what she'd named the fat ewe that was her favourite of the entire menagerie. The ewe baa'd hello, flicking a stubby tail. She'd grown fond of the rotund ruminant and had been sneaking her extra rations.

Once, Dimples had filched two of Henry's wondrous biscuits from Ailish's lunch and immediately loved the delicacy, especially with a spoon of molasses drizzled on top. The ewe was always nuzzling Ailish for the sweet treat, but it was hard to come by as she had to beg it from the kitchen. Henry said she could have one or two buns and a dollop of molasses as it would all end up in the same place anyway.

As Ailish let the ewe lick the last morsel from her palm, she looked around. The breeze had stiffened and white caps were forming on the rolling ocean swells.

She saw Dalton near the stern, wielding a massive wrench, almost as long as her, as easily as he would a fly-swatter. The sharp edge of the wrench glinted in the bruised light as Dalton manipulated one of the many wheels in the piece of machinery. He was totally engrossed, seeming oblivious to everything but his task.

Ailish decided now was her chance. If she was caught, she'd say she was taking the eggs to the galley and got lost. She sidled out of the sheep pen and ran toward the hatch that led belowdecks, slipping the basket over her arm and grabbing the map out of the pocket in her breeches as she went. Hurrying as fast as she could, she made her way to the crew's quarters and hopefully, Dalton's lair.

She checked the map, then the numbers of the cabins as she passed each one, 302, 303, there it was, 304! Then she spied something she hadn't thought about. A keyhole... and where there was a keyhole, there had to be a key. She turned the handle but the door was securely bolted.

"Bilge rats!" she cursed.

"I thought you didn't like the little rodents?"

Ailish whirled around. "Davy!" She clutched a hand to her breast, trying to steady her pounding heart. "You may as well shoot me as scare me to death! What are you doing here?"

"Charlie and me are knocking off for the day and I was on my way to the cargo hold when I caught sight of you and thought I'd see how the search was coming along."

She blew out a puff of air that sent her ragged hair flying back from her forehead. "I am glad to see you, but you could have warned me the blasted cabin would be locked!"

"I thought you'd figure it out for yourself. That Jack tar is a thief – he thinks like a thief and would worry there were others like him about. He probably sleeps with one eye open."

"That still doesn't help me to get in. Do you know where I can get a key?"

"Maybe in the purser's office, but the master keys would be…"

Ailish finished the sentence for him. "…locked up!"

A thought flashed into her brain. "Locked doors are such a nuisance…" she said absently, glancing around and then a wide smile blossomed on her face. "But I'm too close to be defeated now."

Setting the egg basket on the floor, she hurried to a toolbox that was tucked beneath the stairs. Rummaging inside, she was rewarded with exactly what she needed: a piece of thin wire. "Perfect!" she breathed as she returned to Dalton's door.

Davy frowned. "What's that for?"

"Some months ago, me and my da met a magician, Manfred the Magnificent, travelling to the same fair we were bound for. Da struck up a friendship and after a day of performing for the crowds, we'd all sit around a turf fire and the conjurer would show me tricks, one of them being how to open a locked box with a simple magic spell... and a convenient piece of wire."

Davy nodded his head appreciatively, and Ailish set to work.

Wiggling the wire in the keyhole as she'd been taught, she mumbled the magic spell for extra luck and was rewarded when the lock clicked open. With a fast check to make sure no one was about, Ailish turned the knob.

"We're in!" she chirped gleefully, but at that moment, another cabin door at the end of the corridor rattled.

"Get inside quick!" Davy ordered hastily. "I'll do a little bit of magic of my own and then meet you later!"

Ailish scooped the egg basket before ducking into Dalton's room, then closed and locked the door behind her. As she did so, the light in the passageway went out. Without the lights, it was as black as a tomb down here.

She heard a sailor loudly cursing the darkness, then a thin strip of light reappeared under the door once more. Was this Davy's "little bit of magic"? Ailish thought it most impressive. Mr. Jones was a luminary genius if he could manipulate the gaslights with such ease.

She placed her egg basket on top of the chiffonier and turned up the interior lamp fastened to the cabin wall. Dalton's quarters smelled of mouldy socks, rotting food and, she wrinkled her nose, a long-unwashed sweaty body. As she searched, she took extra pains to put everything back exactly as she'd found it. There was no sense in letting the villain know she'd been there.

She looked in drawers and under the mattress, no jewel-encrusted golden horse. She checked inside Dalton's duffle bag and inspected his sea locker, still nothing. The only place left in the sparsely furnished cabin was the closet.

Pulling the double doors open, she found the closet stuffed to overflowing with shirts and pants, along with a couple of coats and even a fancy bowler hat which sat proudly on the top shelf. Cluttering the floor were a pair of tall rubber Wellington boots for wet weather and three pairs of shoes. Who on earth owned *three* pairs of shoes?

She turned the shoes upside down and shook them, then reached inside the Wellingtons, which was disgusting, but the precious horse was not to be found.

A noise in the corridor made her stop. Ailish could hear voices talking loudly and then the unthinkable – the sound of a key in the lock.

Dalton was at the door!

Panic! What should she do? Where could she hide? She ran to the lamp and extinguished it, then leapt into the closet, pulling the doors shut behind her. Squeezing as far back into the corner as possible, she waited. There were louvers in the doors and she was able to peek out and see her nemesis as he stomped into the room.

"We're in for a blow and that's for sure, Jimmy. Let me get my foul weather gear." He called to a crewman in the hallway.

He was here for his raincoat and boots! Ailish looked down at the Wellingtons at her feet and felt around for the oilskin coat. She pushed the boots to the front of the closet and quietly slid the coat near the centre of the closet opening, hoping that he was in a hurry and wouldn't rummage around for anything else.

She watched breathlessly as he moved toward the closet. It was then that her eye fell on the chiffonier. Sitting proudly on top of the dresser was her basket of eggs!

If he saw them, she would never get out of here alive.

Ailish shrank back against the wall as the door was yanked open.

"Get a move on, Rufus. I'm due topside!" An impatient voice shouted from the passageway.

Dalton grabbed the boots and slid the oilskins from their wooden hanger. "Yeah, yeah, hold your horses," he snarled back. "It's as cold as an icehouse tonight and I can't find my blasted sweater."

Ailish felt the scratchy wool against her cheek. She was smack up against the very garment he was searching for! She dared not breathe. As stealthily as possible, she nudged the sweater toward his big, groping fist.

"Got it!" he called, yanking it out of the closet and slamming the door.

Ailish peered through the slats praying he didn't spot the egg basket. The light from the hall lamps cast a wan illumination into the room. Dalton had not bothered to light the gas lamp on the wall, which was good as to do that, he would have to push the egg basket out of the way.

She watched as he hastily pulled on the sweater and boots, then dragged the jacket over everything and hurried out of the cabin.

Sighing with relief, Ailish edged out of the closet. Her stomach was tight as a French corset. Her hands trembled as she pushed the louvered door closed behind her and her head felt odd from holding her breath. That had been too close and it had all been for nothing. She still didn't have the wonderful horse.

10

Cabin Boy Overboard

BEFORE DELIVERING THE EGGS, AILISH TOOK A DETOUR to the hold to tell Davy about the dismal outcome of their latest adventure and also let him know about the meeting with Paddy later. In her excitement at breaking into Dalton's cabin she'd forgotten, but when she arrived in the hold, he was nowhere around. Disappointed, she scribbled a note and left it on their favourite packing case.

With a sigh, she decided she'd better report in to Dalton or he'd wonder where she'd been all this time and start questioning her. She dropped the eggs by the galley and then moved on to the hatchway leading topside, but when she pushed it open, she gasped.

In the short time she'd been below, the world had darkened into a nightmare of thunder and water. A black pall extinguished any light the setting sun may have shared and the sea was now filled with towering cliffs of boiling grey waves.

Icy rain slashed her with razor sharp daggers, instantly soaking her thin clothes and if she hadn't been holding onto the hatch, the unexpected blast of wind would have blown her down. Within seconds, her hair dripped and her body felt like a giant icicle. She wished Davy had a sailors' pea coat in that locker of his as she could surely use it now.

A violent shiver wracked Ailish as she surveyed the ship. Everywhere, shadowy figures of men ran to secure stray items the wind had stolen and tossed around with careless abandon. This was no place for her.

She was about to turn and head back to her stateroom to ride out the storm when she caught a glimpse of ghostly white movement at the stern of the ship. Wiping the rain from her eyes, Ailish looked more closely and was surprised to see it was Dimples. The foolish animal was wandering loose on the deck! In this gale, she'd be washed overboard and no one would notice.

Ailish immediately sprang into action, struggling against the fierce wind and rain as she groped her way toward the wayward ewe. The deck had become slick and she had trouble finding her footing. She flinched as a bright bolt of lightning sliced through the sky telling her the storm was far from abating.

"Dimples!" she called. "Come here, you silly sheep!" It was then that Ailish noticed something very odd indeed.

Dimples had lost weight.

In fact, she was positively skinny!

Then Ailish saw the small bundle curled up on the deck. It was a lamb, a wee, newborn lamb. No wonder

Dimples had been so fat. She'd had a baby and must have tried to get as far away from the rest of the flock as was possible on a ship.

Ailish wrapped her arms around the soaking sheep. "Dimples, my girl, your timing is terrible."

Dimples looked up at her with big brown eyes and made a chuckling sound deep in her throat. Her tone sounded a tiny bit smug and a lot unrepentant.

Carefully, Ailish scooped up the tiny lamb in her arms as she tried to reassure both mother and baby. "Come on you two. We're going back to the pen. You'll be warm and safe in the stable."

As she turned to struggle back down the deck, something out of place caught her eye. She squinted to clear her vision.

Lying on top of the automatic release mechanism was the huge wrench she'd seen Dalton wielding earlier. It was precariously close to the edge of the housing. If the movement of the ship caused it to slip, the wrench would fall into the machine smashing the complicated gears and wheels and releasing the cable to free fall into the sea!

Ailish hurried to the stable and tucked the lamb safely into a warm dry corner, laying it on the straw, where Dimples contentedly nuzzled her newborn.

The wind was a howling demon as she searched the deck for someone strong enough to lift the tool. She caught sight of Dalton's hulking form, swathed in his foul weather gear, high above on the catwalk that spanned the wide deck.

Not her first choice, but there was no time to find another deckhand. Ailish called out to him. Her words were carried away with the shrieking wind. Scrambling closer, she called again; still it was no good. The clang and bang of the cable machines as they laboured was the only noise loud enough to be heard over the roar of the storm.

With trepidation, she started up the rain-slicked ladder that led to the treacherous catwalk. The force of the wind buffeted her and only by grabbing the metal railing with both hands and pulling herself up rung by rung was she able to climb. Once at the top, the tempest ripped at her mercilessly.

Ailish dragged herself forward. "Mr. Dalton! Mr. Dalton! You've got to come with me!" She grabbed his arm to get his attention. "You left a large tool on the release mechanism and it's going to fall in!"

He turned on her, furious. "I did no such thing! Loose talk like that will get you killed. Now, get off me, you poor excuse for a powder monkey, or I'll flay you alive." With a mighty swing of his arm, he lifted Ailish off her feet and sent her flying, as easily as one would flick away a pesky gnat.

She desperately tried to grab something to hold onto, but the railing was slippery and she fell, tumbling down the steps and hitting the deck below with a hard thump that knocked the wind out of her. The force of the landing sent her rolling out of control across the rain-soaked planking directly toward the open edge of the ship.

It all happened in an instant.

Screaming, Ailish felt herself flung into the frigid darkness.

Whirling and spinning, she plummeted downward, dread closed her throat as she waited to slam into the icy waves far below.

With a bone-jarring *whump*, she landed, not on the hard surface of the sea, but on a solid wooden ledge. Scrabbling with frozen fingertips, Ailish managed to grip a cleat nailed to the structure and hang on. She groaned as she sucked air back into battered lungs. Terror seized her anew as the waves, like deadly dragon talons, clawed at her each time the ship rolled and her precarious perch dipped closer to the iron-grey ocean.

She'd fallen onto the shroud of one of the huge paddle wheels that flanked either side of the *Great Eastern's* hull. The ship seemed to sail smoothly enough on the deck, but here, suspended so far over the churning water, she was tossed about like a rag doll with each wave surge. Spray as cold as witch's spit made everything slimy.

Her fingertips grew bloody as she desperately clung to the small wooden board attached to the paddle wheel housing. How long she could hang on, she wasn't sure. Ailish struggled to get closer to the side of the ship and away from the edge of the narrow platform. One thing was certain; it wouldn't be long before the sea claimed her.

"Help! Down here on the paddlewheel!" she yelled,

then listened intently, hopelessly, for an answering cry. But all she heard was the storm's unceasing wail. To Ailish's desperate ears, it sounded like Davy's voice calling out, a lamentation by her graveside. "Please save me!" she shouted back into the dark face of the storm, knowing there was no one there.

She thought of her da and tears, as salty as the sea-water drenching her, trickled down her cheeks. She hadn't found his magical golden horse. Her father would spend the rest of his days wondering what had happened to her. Rufus Dalton would never tell. She realized with a pang that she wanted to say so many things to her da, like how much she loved him and that they were a great team. Now she wouldn't get the chance.

The water was near freezing and Ailish soon felt a numbness stealing through her entire body. She laid her head on her arms, too weak to do more than wait for the inevitable.

"*O'Connor! Up here!*"

She must be near death, she decided. She could hear God calling her name.

"Lad, look up!"

Ailish slowly lifted her head. Someone *had* called her, and it wasn't God!

"Here! I'm here!" She rasped weakly as she blinked, straining to see through the blinding rain. Blurrily, she could make out the face of Paddy Whelan, leaning over the ship's side with a rope and round life preserver.

"I'll drop this down to you, lad. Put the ring over your head and I'll draw you up!"

She nodded, no breath left to answer.

With sluggish fingers, she grabbed at the preserver and dragged it over her head and under her arms. "Pull!" she called.

Paddy hauled on the rope. Ailish held tightly as she was lifted off her aerie only to be dangled perilously over the dark sea below. She closed her eyes, not daring to look down.

She swayed and twirled, holding on with the last of her strength, then after what seemed an eternity, she felt Paddy take hold and gather her to him. She was safe, safe at last. Death moaned in defeat and fled as great wracking sobs welled up from her chest.

"How did you know I was here?" she hiccupped, wiping her snotty nose on her sleeve.

"I went below to meet you and found the note you'd written and beside it, one in the dust telling me to come to the starboard paddlewheel. I heard you calling and looked over the edge. I don't mind admitting, I was scared when I saw you stuck down there."

"That makes two of us, Paddy." Her head spun with relief. Had the strange wailing she'd heard been real? Had Davy called to her? Surely, it had only been the wind.

But it must have been her friend. Seeing the desperate situation, had he realized it would take more than he could do to save her? Had he left the second note sending Paddy, who was bigger and stronger, to rescue her while he... what? While he went to round up a posse to join in the rescue? She glanced about for him, then like a thunderbolt, she remembered what else was about to happen. "Paddy, we have to stop a disaster! There's a huge wrench going to fall into the automatic release mechanism. The machine will be destroyed!"

Paddy didn't argue. He took her arm and together they struggled back to the large piece of intricate machinery. They both spotted the cumbersome tool at the moment it finished its last slide and disappeared into the housing. Immediately, an ominous grinding sound started up.

"It's going to seize at any second. We've got to get that wrench out!" Paddy raced to the wheels and reached into the shrieking apparatus. Ailish watched helplessly as her friend tried to free the tool. After several futile moments, Paddy shook his head. One of his arms was bloody from tearing vainly at the wrench. "It's no good. The blasted thing is already wedged in. If I could pry the gears..."

Ailish saw a lifeboat hanging from a davit against the outside of the hull and ran to it, then faltered, staring down. Sixty feet below, the hungry sea reared up as if trying for a second chance to devour her. Terror squeezed her in its paralyzing fist and her muscles refused to obey. "No, no, no!" she hissed through clenched teeth, fighting to regain control. Desperately, she wanted to run and hide, but the cable could be destroyed and that was bigger than her fear.

Taking a deep breath, she scrambled onto the boat as it hung suspended over the ocean far below. The wind rocked and shook the small craft as she released one end of the tarpaulin and climbed inside. It was dark but dry under the cover, and she felt around for what she needed. At last her fingers closed on her prize. Grabbing the oak oar, she clambered back to the deck and then hurried to Paddy.

"Use this!"

Paddy took the stout length of wood and wedged it under the wrench, then leaned on it with all his might. With a crack, the wooden oar splintered in two, but not before the wrench popped out of the wheel assembly.

"Paddy, you did it!" Ailish cheered, swiping at the rain in her eyes.

"What's going on here?" a harsh voice growled.

Ailish and Paddy whirled to see Dalton and several of his men standing behind them. In the eerie light from the storm, they appeared menacing gargoyles and Ailish took a step backward as a wash of pure menace rolled off Dalton and engulfed her.

"The Fenian scum is trying to sabotage the cable! You'll hang for this, Whelan," Dalton snarled. "Unless you've decided to take my offer…"

"You never give up, do you, Dalton? The answer's still no. Now, shove off." Paddy turned to check the damaged wheel.

"You drove that spike through the cable and when that didn't work, you decided to try again tonight. No man aboard will see it differently!"

In the wavering glow from the lone electric lamp high on the mast, Dalton looked a true demon. Summoning her courage again, Ailish stepped forward. "No, Paddy's trying to save the cable!" she shouted. "You left a wrench lying over the machinery today and it fell in during the storm. I tried to warn you, but you wouldn't listen. Instead, you almost killed me and caused a cable disaster!"

The smirk on Dalton's face faltered and his men saw it. She realized she'd committed a grave error. Not only had she caught Dalton making a careless blunder, she had exposed him in front of his men.

His eyes grew as cold as the icy Atlantic. "A bald-faced lie! You and Whelan set this up."

He lunged for her but Paddy stepped between. "You're the problem here, Dalton. Don't blame O'Connor."

Ailish could see doubt cross the men's faces. It was hard to lead an army if your troops thought you were incompetent and now, the seeds had been planted. She almost felt sorry for the fiend, almost... but not quite. Anyone could make a mistake, but the right thing to do was to own up to it and try to make amends. Dalton had done neither.

"What's the problem, Mr. Dalton?"

Ailish turned to see the tall figure of Cyrus Field striding through the torrential downpour. "Mr. Field!

Thank goodness." She rushed to his side. "Sir... Paddy freed a wrench that had fallen into the wheels and now Mr. Dalton is accusing him of attempting to wreck the automatic release mechanism!"

"The Irishman's up to no good, sir." The crew chief interrupted. "We found him doing his best to sabotage the cable in the hopes the storm would hide his tampering."

Ailish looked at Dalton in surprise. He was fast on his feet, that was sure.

The soft-spoken gentleman looked about the rain-washed deck and saw the wrench and the broken oar. "Did anyone actually see Mr. Whelan attempting to destroy the machine?"

Dalton didn't answer.

"Then did anyone see him trying to save the machine?" Cyrus Field asked.

"Yes sir. I did." Ailish spoke up as she shot Dalton a meaningful glare. "Paddy is not the one at fault here."

"You're not going to take a stowaway Irish brat's word are you, Mr. Field?" Dalton asked in his gravelly voice. "I'll wager my rum ration they're in this together."

"In America, Mr. Dalton, a man is innocent until proven guilty. I see no reason to dispute Mr. O'Connor's word. It appears some inept sailor left the wrench where it could wreak havoc. I think we narrowly averted a disaster here this evening." Mr. Field turned and walked away into the rainy night.

Dalton jabbed Paddy with his finger. "That does it, Whelan. You signed your own death warrant." Then he and his men strode back down Oxford Street.

Ailish feared he meant what he'd said and Paddy's life was now in real danger.

11

FENIANS ABOARD!

SATURDAY MORNING ARRIVED WITH A CLOUDLESS SKY and air that smelled washed and clean. Ailish had decided to steer clear of Mr. Dalton for as long as possible and was busy playing with Dimples and her new lamb when Paddy walked up, swinging a basket brimming with freshly baked buns.

"I'm supposed to be working in the cable tank today, but since I'm injured from last night's adventure," he showed her his bandaged arm, "I asked Dalton if I could work up on deck instead. He wasn't going to let me, but Mr. Field was there, saw my wounds, and suggested that would be prudent. I thought Dalton was going to choke he was so angry, so I decided I'd best leave."

Paddy's face became serious. "I wanted to say thank you for what you did last night, O'Connor. I'm not used to anyone sticking up for me." He handed her the basket. "These are for your pet."

Ailish beamed. "Dimples, say thank you."

"Baaaa," the ewe obediently replied.

"You too, Rainbow."

The lamb gave a small bleat.

She fed two of the warm buns to the polite ewe, and then stroked Rainbow's velvet ears. "I said nothing but the truth, and anyway, it's me who should be thanking you. You saved my life."

Paddy folded his arms. "I might not have made it in time if you hadn't written me that note."

Ailish shook her head. "That wasn't me. Davy must have left it and then gone in search of more help, but I haven't been to the machinery hold today to ask him about it. Charlie's probably got him working again. He's an amazing fellow." She didn't care anymore how obstinate and frustrating Davy could be; she trusted him and wanted their friendship to continue.

"I didn't think there was anyone down there slaving except swabbies like me." Paddy smiled. "I'm glad I could be of service. I'd say we make a fine pair."

Ailish hugged the tiny sheep. "Isn't Rainbow beautiful?" She said, not expecting an answer. "His fleece is so soft. I can already see him running and doing little sheepy things in a sunny meadow in Newfoundland."

Paddy looked from the lamb to Ailish. "O'Connor, you do know why these animals are on board, don't you?"

Ailish stopped cuddling Rainbow. She really hadn't thought much about it, and then with a horrifying lurch, Henry the cook's words came back to her. He said he hadn't minded giving Dimples the buns and molasses because it would end up in the same place anyway.

The same place – *on the table!* They were fresh meat!

The animals were on board to feed the crew. "No, this can't be! Paddy, we have to save Dimples and Rainbow. Please. We can't let them end up as, as," she swallowed, "mutton stew and lamb chops!"

Paddy burst out laughing in that big way he had as Ailish anxiously looked from ewe to lamb and then back to Paddy.

"Oh, stop looking like that, laddie. Dalton wants me in the tank for some reason, so give me a half hour and then we'll go see Henry and perhaps, with a small incentive," he winked at her, "our cook could be persuaded to go with roast chicken and not lamb stew."

Paddy disappeared for a long while, then true to his word, came to get her. His timing was perfect as Ailish was about to stop for a bite to eat.

"Our crew chief's a nasty one, but no quitter," Paddy said as they made their way belowdecks. "He wanted me in the tank so he could demand my money again or he'd expose me. He said the incident last night would prove my guilt, or that's how everyone on board would see it."

Ailish knew the lengths the man would go to. "I'm amazed at how hard Mr. Dalton works for other people's fortunes. Come on, we have to plead for a stay of execution for Dimples and son."

They spoke to the cook and though Ailish couldn't prove it, she was sure money was exchanged as Henry assured her the pets would be safe. His only stipulation was that she had to take them with her once they reached shore as he didn't want to explain to the captain how these two escaped the menu.

— – • – —

AILISH AND PADDY HAD NO SOONER RETURNED TO THE deck when the air was rent by the sound they all dreaded – the terrible gong. She shuddered, wanting to cover her ears to block out the ominous tolling.

The ship sprang to life. Orders were shouted and men manned machines as they braced for what would come next.

"Stay here," Paddy ordered, then ran to help.

Anxiously Ailish waited the long hours it took to slow the ship, cut the cable and transfer it to the bow, before reeling it back in. She heard the men say it would be a difficult time as there was more than two thousand fathoms of water under the ship's keel and four tons of cable trying to break free.

She went to the testing caboose and eased inside. She'd visited the darkened hideout several times and knew the operators if not by sight, then by voice. "It's me, O'Connor," she announced into the blackness. It took her eyes a moment to adjust to the low light conditions, but then she saw the dim shapes of the two silent operators, sitting like statues in front of their machines. "Any chance the signal will start again like it did before?" she asked hopefully.

"There's not been the tiniest spark," one of them said gloomily.

"Joe's right, lad. It's dead for sure this time." The other operator agreed, not hiding the trepidation in his voice. "Not so much as a blink."

"Don't give up yet," Ailish offered hopefully. "I heard Professor Thomson can work miraculous cures. You'll be flashing your ghost messages back to Ireland before you know it."

"You're a good lad, O'Connor," Joe the operator said. "That's the right attitude."

The atmosphere brightened a little and Ailish went to the galley to fetch hot coffee and sandwiches for the telegraph operators who sat so patiently in the darkness while the fate of the mission lay twelve thousand feet below.

As she walked back to the testing caboose, she passed a group of sailors and overheard one mention he'd heard the tap-tap-tapping of a hammer belowdecks.

"I'm telling you, it's the riveter! That devil's at it again, all right. Makin' an infernal racket down there, he is." He made the sign to ward off evil.

Ailish thought this was uncalled for. Pounding rivets couldn't help being a noisy job! And calling Charlie a devil was mean spirited. He seemed a decent enough chap, letting Davy visit almost anytime she was in the hold.

Ailish delivered the food and stayed to talk with the two men who manned the darkened room. They chatted and swapped stories, laughing as Ailish drew on the wealth of bad jokes she'd heard her father tell. This made her feel better as every time she thought of the weight on these men's shoulders, she was amazed they could remain in such good spirits. Their judgment on the cable's signal had the power to bring either cheers of triumph or the cries of defeat to the entire world.

— – • — —

It was Monday before one of the crew, carefully scraping the thick grey sludge off the dead wire, discovered what had caused the fault.

"Here, I've got it! Get the captain!" he called as men hurriedly moved to where the sailor was inspecting the damaged cable.

Rufus Dalton stood looking very pleased with himself and Ailish nudged Paddy in the ribs. "He looks like a man with a fat pay packet in his pocket. I have a bad feeling about this."

Moments later Captain Anderson, Mr. Canning, Professor Thomson and Cyrus Field assembled around the sailor who had raised the alarm.

"Full house," Ailish murmured. "Darn near every mucky-muck we have on board."

They conferred for some time; then the captain motioned Rufus Dalton over and spoke to him. The group continued talking as Dalton pointed to the cable releasing mechanism that had come so close to disaster and they all nodded their heads solemnly, concurring with whatever it was Dalton was saying.

Around her, Ailish could here the dreaded word being murmured – *sabotage*.

A fresh knot tightened in her stomach. She was sure Dalton was telling them Paddy had been trying to wreck the machine. She doubted her word would hold much sway now.

Captain Anderson turned his attention to Ailish and she had the strong urge to run. "O'Connor, was Mr. Whelan with you Saturday morning, before the fault occurred?"

"Yes, sir," she stammered, hating the limelight.

"And where did he say he was supposed to be working?"

"In the cable tank sir, but because of his injury, he'd asked Mr. Dalton if he could work on deck instead."

"So he was not in the tank at any time before the fault occurred." The captain looked at Dalton. "This means he couldn't have sabotaged the cable."

"He could have done it. It would only take a moment." Dalton said. "Maybe he slipped away when no one was watching."

The crowd murmured agreement, eager for a target.

Captain Anderson addressed Ailish again. "And at no time did Mr. Whelan go belowdecks?"

Ailish was about to say Paddy was with her topside all the time, but then she thought of him leaving to see Dalton. She felt as though she were betraying her countryman when she answered. "Only for a few minutes, Captain. He said he had to go to the ..." her words trailed off.

"Did he go to the cable tank?" the captain pressed.

"Yes, sir," Ailish said in a small voice, then went on quickly, "Mr. Dalton wanted to see him."

"I gave no such order!" Dalton lied, then pointed at Paddy. "He pretended illness to get out of working in the tank so he would have an alibi, then he slunk back like the dog he is and wrecked the cable! And what's more, Whelan was in the tank the day of the first fault! The Fenian traitor should pay!"

Ailish's throat went dry. Dalton wanted Paddy to pay, all right, but not in the way everyone else would think. It was a little disconcerting that Paddy was in the hold or unaccounted for when all the faults had occurred. If she didn't know better, she too would have suspected the kind Irishman. Now there were shouts from the crew to hang the traitor and throw him overboard.

Cyrus Field stepped forward. "There's no proof Mr. Whelan is the saboteur. Being Irish does not make him a Fenian."

"It makes him the most likely candidate!" someone from the crowd shouted. "The rest of us are loyal to Queen Victoria and the Empire and we want the cable to succeed!"

The American calmly continued. "Our traitor could be an Englishman who sympathizes with the Irish cause and is using Paddy Whelan as a convenient scapegoat."

"Everyone here knows you can't trust an Irishman!" Dalton shouted. "We won't let the cable be stopped by one man even if we have to deal with matters ourselves!"

Captain Anderson held up his hands and called for silence. "Gentleman, I can confirm that the cable shorted because of a two-inch spike driven through its heart, exactly as was done previously. We have concluded that this is indeed sabotage and those most likely responsible would be the Irish group known as the Fenians. However, I shall not arrest a man because of hysteria and without any evidence to convict him of the crime." The grumbling grew louder as the captain continued. "Go back to your posts and be diligent. If you see anyone acting suspiciously, report it immediately to Mr. Dalton or myself."

The crowd dispersed with mutterings and thinly veiled threats as to what would happen when they caught the traitor.

Dalton, trailed by several of his burly gang, sidled up to Paddy. "The crew seem a might upset," he said with a smirk. "What do you think would happen if anyone saw that picture now, Whelan? Without my protection, you could have a terrible, *and deadly,* accident." He shouldered past Paddy and left with his men.

"This is not looking good, O'Connor." Paddy said, watching Dalton leave. "I think you should stay away from me for a while, in case my dear friend Rufus arranges that accident he was talking about. I wouldn't want you to get hurt."

"I'll not let that mad dog chase me away. I'm not afraid of Rufus Dalton." Ailish's words sounded braver than she felt.

"Then you're a fool, O'Connor. Dalton is a dangerous man and a lad like you is no match for him."

Ailish thought of how she'd outwitted him so far and it gave her confidence. "We can handle him."

"There is no *we*, O'Connor! This is not a game for a wet-behind-the-ears boy. Stay away from me! I've all I can deal with looking after myself. I don't want to babysit you!"

Ailish was about to protest, but Paddy stalked away before she could say another word.

12

A CALL TO BATTLE!

.-- .... --- ....-... ..... - --.-.. . -. .-.-.--...

"THEY FOUND THE FAULT, DAVY." AILISH SAGGED AGAINST a wooden packing case. "Paddy's been accused of being a Fenian and driving spikes through the cable. You should have seen the crew. They turned into an ugly, blood-thirsty mob."

"But you said he wasn't the one. Are you still so sure?" Davy asked, a mocking light in his sea-green eyes. He was sitting cross-legged on top of his usual crate and, in the hazy light with dust motes dancing in the air, he appeared an apparition from a mystical world.

She thought of how things looked – very bad; then she thought of the feeling she got from Paddy – very good.

"He's innocent. This whole sabotage thing makes no sense." She ran her fingers through her chopped hair. Her da's smiling face flashed into her mind. She remembered once when she and her mother had done their hair in exactly the same style, twining flowers into the compli-cated braids; then, laughing, they'd shown him. He'd said he was a blessed man with two of the most beautiful colleens in Ireland to call his own. Blinking rapidly to clear the image from her mind, she returned her attention to Davy.

"At first, I thought Dalton was bluffing to make Paddy give him the money, threatening to show the captain the incriminating picture, but then the faults began. After what happened on deck, that picture would put the nails in Paddy's coffin for sure. No one would believe he was only at the meeting to have a listen." She shook her head. "The timing of the faults is so blasted convenient. When I first came on board, I overheard Dalton threatening Paddy and within hours the first fault happened, and then during the storm, I made the mistake of exposing Dalton as careless in front of his gang and Paddy defended me. Again, Dalton threatened him, and bang! We have another spike through the cable. It's hard to believe it was coincidence. I wouldn't put it past Dalton to have arranged the faults to put pressure on Paddy. After all, eighty pounds is a whopping lot of money."

Agitated, she paced up and down. "What scares me is how Dalton is encouraging the men to take the law into their own hands and arrange an accident for the Fenian, who everyone now thinks is Paddy. Dalton saw to that." She halted her march. "And if the crew doesn't toss him overboard, Dalton will give the picture to the captain who will haul Paddy away for treason. Either way that thief will scoop the money! A dead man can't complain someone stole his fortune."

The more she thought about it, the worse it looked. "I've got a bad feeling we'll soon be reading about 'the wealthy Rufus Dalton' in the *Irish Times*."

"The very wealthy Rufus Dalton – he'd have your statue too. This is a dusty business," Davy agreed.

"Dusty? It's downright dirty!" Ailish cried, leaning on the box again. Sometimes she thought Davy enjoyed all this intrigue a little too much. She sighed. "The famous missing two-pound horse... Since our search of Dalton's room didn't turn up turnips, do you think he could have put it in the ship's safe?"

"Nay." A crease furrowed Davy's brow. "If he had, the loose-lipped grog hounds who work for the purser would blab it about for sure."

"Dalton is the only one who knows where that horse is." Ailish idly picked at a splinter on the crate as she thought. "It's him who'll have to lead me to the stash. The *Great Eastern* is too mammoth to search deck by deck, room by room and time is growing short. Paddy told me the cable-laying will go much faster as soon as we get closer to Newfoundland. Once we reach port, Dalton will abscond with Paddy's money, sell my da's horse, and then disappear for good."

One solution popped into her head. "We could follow him around the clock. I could take the first watch and you could trail him while I'm sleeping."

Davy shook his head. "Unless he had some reason to go and check his treasure, all we'd end up doing is watching him as he worked, ate and slept. You already did that and it turned up ashes. I don't go on deck unless it's for someone incredible and extraordinary and Dalton is neither. Besides, Charlie's a gruff one and keeps me too busy."

He cocked his head. "Speak of the devil! There's his lordship calling me again."

Ailish looked around. She hadn't heard anything, and then there it was. The sound of a hammer blow striking iron. Far away like a distant echo. Keeping a ship this size from springing a leak was surely a full time job.

"Ails, have you thought about what would happen should you be a clever girl and find your horse? No one is going to believe an Irish stowaway owns a valuable statue like that."

Ailish hadn't thought about it, but Davy was right. And she had no doubt Dalton would get his cronies to back up a claim that it was his. Things looked bleak.

An image of her ma and da came into her mind again. Ailish knew their life had been hard, but her parents never gave up no matter how steep the mountain. They simply kept at it. Her da always said, "It's during the tough times that your mettle is tested. Anyone can be brave when your belly's full and the roof don't leak."

These were her tough times. She straightened. She was Ailish O'Connor, and she was not going to give up and let Dalton win!

"We have to turn the tables on Rufus Dalton." She smiled. "I think lashings of revenge are called for, plus I plan on winning this war. To win completely means I have to find my da's fabulous horse *and* clear Paddy of suspicion. That's a challenge worthy of an O'Connor and maybe, if I really am a clever girl…" she had a twinkle in her eye now, "I can do both at once."

13

SETTING A TRAP
FOR A RAT

AILISH SPENT THE NEXT DAY TRYING TO COME UP WITH a plan. Not any old plan would do: it had to be brilliant and cunning. She couldn't out-muscle Dalton, but she was pretty sure she could outsmart him. The question was, how?

As Paddy had predicted, the speed of the cable-laying increased. They were now only seven hundred miles from Newfoundland and approaching the Grand Banks, the finest fishing grounds in the whole world. Compared to the depths they had traversed, the Grand Banks was shallow water for the *Great Eastern* to lay her precious cargo.

After checking on Dimples and Rainbow that night, Ailish went to bed still without an answer. The stakes were so very high. Her da always said if you want to catch a rat, you have to bait the trap. Then he would add with a chuckle, "Of course, it doesn't hurt to think like the little rodent either!" She was going to have to be as devious and deceptive as Dalton. As she drifted off to sleep, her mind whirled with a thousand thoughts.

Wednesday morning, Ailish awoke from a vivid dream that had left her feeling excited and eager. Woven into that vaporous landscape of grey mist and black dust had been the blueprint for her master plan. She could remember it all with crystal clarity, especially the parts with Davy. He'd seemed so real in her slumber world and what was truly strange was that in her dream, Davy had held out his hands to her and she'd taken them, holding tight as a wonderful warm tingle made her want to laugh and dance. She had to admit, he was special. She'd never dreamt about a boy before, ever!

In the crew's mess, Ailish indulged herself in a large and hearty breakfast, noticing that she was putting on weight from the regular and abundant meals. Her borrowed clothes were becoming a little tight. Next, she stopped by the testing caboose for a quick visit with the lads before going on deck. Moving about the huge ship, she could sense that tension was still running high. It was like living in a powder keg with Rufus Dalton waiting to light the fuse.

She stood at the bow, watching a pod of dolphins jump and dive in their ocean playground. As they raced ahead of the ship, the sleek animals would leap from the water in a joyous display, then fall back, their splashes creating a brilliant rainbow in the bright morning sun.

Her dream plan would be dangerous to implement, but if she were going to get Dalton to lead her to the horse, she needed something daring. If anything went wrong, it would spell disaster not only for her, but for Paddy, because despite his warnings to stay away, she would need his help.

The one thing essential for her plan to succeed was smooth sailing from here to Heart's Content. She knew if there were any more problems with the cable, the captain would arrest Paddy, proof or no proof. It was only because Captain Anderson was such a fair man that he hadn't thrown the big Irishman in the brig already.

There was no time like the present to put her plan into action. She waved goodbye to the dolphins, then went to find Paddy.

After asking several crewmen if they'd seen him, Ailish finally discovered he was in the machinery storage hold. She found him near where she always met Davy. He was hoisting a large wheel out of a box and looked up when she walked over.

"I told you to stay away from me." He set the wheel down on a dolly then wiped the sweat from his forehead and added kindly, "It's for your own good, boy."

Ailish smiled. "I know you're only looking out for me, but I have a way we can solve both our problems and sink Dalton in the bargain." She clambered up on what she now thought of as Davy and Ailish's crate and sat swinging her leg.

He raised a quizzical eyebrow at her. "Both our problems? I'm the one he's going to throw to the sharks. What dark deed has he done to you?"

This was the opening she'd waited for. "Well now, Mr. Whelan, I'm glad you asked. Do you remember several days ago, I tried to tell you why I had to stay on the ship?"

Paddy waited for her to go on.

"It's because I'm following Rufus Dalton. He took something from my da and me in Foilhummerum Bay and I'm here to get it back."

Paddy frowned, and then he studied her face. "There was a young girl on the wharf the morning we sailed. She was looking for Dalton."

Ailish stopped swinging her leg. "That girl was me."

He stepped back. "What are you talking about?"

"She is me. Well, I am her." She began again. "My name is Ailish O'Connor and Rufus Dalton stole a small statue from my family and it's stashed somewhere on the ship. Our future is wrapped up in that horse figurine. My da and I are going to Newfoundland and he's going to be a fisherman and I'll run our grand house and maybe I can go to school and…"

"Whoa! Hang on, lad, I mean lass." He ran his hand rapidly back and forth through his hair as though trying to shake out a confusing problem. "Start at the beginning and for the love of all the saints, go slowly."

She could see Paddy was now thoroughly confused. "Have a seat." She indicated one of the crates. "Davy likes that one." He settled himself and she told him the whole story, including her father's bloody injury, evading Dalton the day she ended up in the sheep pen and the frightening search of the crew chief's smelly room.

"I won't leave this ship without that horse," she concluded, sounding very sure of herself.

Paddy's jaw was set in a firm line. "That Dalton's a thief is no surprise, but the savagery of his attack on your father sickens me. He needs to pay for his misdeeds and return your property. As for me, Dalton knows he has me at the point of his sword. One more problem with the cable and I'll be lynched or in the brig, then there's no one to stand in his way as he steals my inheritance."

She could tell his eyes were gazing into the past when next he spoke.

"The Great Famine nearly wiped out my entire family. Without that money, those few that survived and escaped to Canada will end up in paupers' graves, as surely as the ones who starved to death in Ireland."

"We won't let him rob you too." Ailish took a deep breath and began to lay out her plan. "A little meeting with Mr. Dalton is called for where you say there's rumour someone on board found a treasure – a statue of a golden horse all encrusted with jewels – and that this mystery man plans on selling it as soon as we reach port."

Surprise lit up Paddy's face. "Golden? Jewel-encrusted? That sounds like something Dalton would kill for. I'd say your father had a lucky shamrock to survive that attack. Tell me lass, how did your da come by this treasure?"

"He bought it from a Russian soldier who needed a wee bit of travelling money. He said it was out of the czar's palace in St. Petersburg."

"I can see why the likes of Mr. Dalton would find that irresistible."

"When he hears it's been taken, he'll want to go and check." She looked very pleased with herself. "That's when I follow him to his stash. Once he sees it's there and you're full of malarkey, he'll go back to tell you, probably with his fists," she added apologetically. "When he's talking to you, that's when I take it for real."

"That sounds like it will put your world right." He rubbed his stubbly chin. "But you said this plan would take care of my problem also. How do you propose we do that?"

"Simple. We offer to trade the horse for that incriminating picture out of the newspaper and Dalton's guarantee that he'll tell the lynch mob they have the wrong man."

Paddy shook his head vehemently. "No. You said that statue was all you and your da had to make a better future. I won't let you sacrifice it so I'll be safe."

Ailish felt positively impish when she answered. "Don't worry about that. Dalton forgets this is the *Great Eastern* – the legendary ship that's laying the transatlantic cable from Ireland to Newfoundland! Now let's get started."

14

FOILED AGAIN!

.... --- .-- -- .- -.-- .-..- .. -... -...-.. -.. .- .-.. - --- . ...- ...-.

P ADDY SENT A MESSAGE TO D ALTON THAT IT WAS important they meet in the machinery storage hold. While they waited, Ailish busied herself extinguishing most of the gas lamps so that it was dimly lit and the shadows hard to see through. Not only would this help her spy on the meeting, but the darkness would also hide her when she followed Dalton out of the hold.

They didn't have long to wait.

"Have you found your senses, Whelan?" Dalton asked as he strode in, trailing two large crewmen behind him.

"I never lost them, Rufus, but my fortune isn't what I want to talk to you about, it's yours."

Dalton slouched back against one of the crates. "Is that so? Maybe you better explain yourself."

"It has to do with a certain valuable statue…"

Dalton immediately straightened up. "What the devil are you blathering about?"

"I think you know. A golden horse, decorated with jewels that you procured in Foilhummerum the night we left."

"What nonsense," he scoffed, but there was no conviction in his voice. "Why don't you tell me your story?"

Paddy looked around as though gathering his thoughts. "Let's see. What if the horse that you tucked away here on the ship had been found by a person who immediately recognized its worth? And what if this person had himself hidden it so that he could take it with him when we docked in Newfoundland? I'm guessing this fortunate soul would now be a wealthy gentleman in the making."

Dalton's face went an impressive shade of red and Ailish, watching from behind the safety of several artfully arranged boxes, wondered if his puffed up head was going to explode.

"Who has it?" Dalton raged.

Smiling, Paddy stroked his chin. "Well, now, I'd say you have five hundred suspects, including those lads you brought with you as muscle."

Dalton looked at his henchmen. "We'll get to the bottom of this right now. Keep him here until I get back."

The two enforcers hefted iron pipes threateningly as they moved toward Paddy. Dalton stormed out and Ailish, ghostlike, followed after him.

— - • — —

DALTON LED HER THROUGH THE VAST EXPANSE OF THE ship and down passageways she'd never seen before. Belowdecks was a labyrinth with intersecting hallways, stairs to unknown passages and a dizzying number of doors to who knew where.

Ailish was grateful they were on a ship as she knew no matter how twisted around she became, if she kept going up, eventually, she would be topside and all made clear.

They were deep in the lower decks and the dim lighting, instead of working in her favour, now made it hard to see which way they were going. It was dusty and dirty down here and they were alone. Her footsteps seemed very loud as she trailed after Dalton. She was afraid to move closer as he might discover her following and then he'd... she didn't want to think of what he'd do if he caught her.

Ailish rounded another of the thousand corners, to find Dalton hurrying down a particularly long corridor that opened onto three possible exits. She darted back out of sight and waited to see which of the identical doors he would choose. As she watched, he approached the hatchways at the end of the passage. He reached his large hand out for one of the doors...

"O'Connor, what are you doing skulking around down here, lad?"

With a start, she spun to see Cyrus Field and Captain Anderson approaching.

"Me, Mr. Field? What am I doing down here, sir?" She didn't know what to say, nothing brilliant came to her. She had no choice but to tell the truth. "Actually sir, I'm quite lost. I've never been in this part of the ship

before and I seem to have gotten myself turned about."
Truer words had never been spoken. She had no idea
where she was.

Captain Anderson looked sympathetic. "I know boy,
this ship is as big as a floating city and one needs a guide
to navigate. We only took this black passageway because
it's a shortcut to the bridge. Where were you heading and
we'll give you directions?"

At that moment, Ailish heard the clang of an iron
door banging shut.

The two gentleman stood waiting. Ailish tried to
think of an appropriate answer. "Where was I going…?"
She must sound like a right eejit. She stepped into the
hallway where she'd last seen Dalton. He was gone and
there was no way to tell which of the doors he'd taken.

"I'm going to the machinery storage hold," she said
dejectedly. It had been a good plan – unless you ran into
the captain and a wealthy American. She had failed again
and wherever Dalton had secreted that statue, it would
remain hidden.

15

TREASURE CHEST

FOLLOWING THE CAPTAIN'S DIRECTIONS, AILISH MADE her way from the dank lowest decks where she'd been following Dalton and up to the machinery hold where the henchmen had Paddy. As she navigated, she tried to think of how to fix the mess she was in. She needed a new plan. Unbidden, her mind filled with images of last night's dream. It had seemed so real, so vivid, and in it she had been successful not only in finding the horse, but in clearing Paddy. Now she could do neither.

She turned into the companionway that led to the hold. With a whoof the wind was knocked out of her. Her arms were grabbed so hard she thought they were going to be ripped out of their sockets.

"Why are you following me, boy?"

She looked up into the sweaty, red face of Rufus Dalton. "I'm not following you, sir!" She squeaked. Sadly true, she wasn't any more.

"You're lying! That was you below just now. You've been up to something from the first time I laid eyes on you." He squeezed her arms and she winced in pain.

"No, Mr. Dalton." Her pulse was pounding now. "I was on my way to see Mr. Field and I took a wrong turn. Maybe I was on the same deck as you, but that was merely coincidence. I have to deliver an important message... from Captain Anderson, sir." She hoped this would make him free her. No one interfered with the captain's business.

"I've had it with you, O'Connor."

He roughly thrust her away from him and she smashed into the bulkhead. Pain lanced down her spine.

Dalton pointed a dirty finger at her. "Now, shove off and remember, stop messing where you don't belong."

She inched away from him, her aching back hugging the wall, then turned and fled up the stairs. Rubbing her sore arms, she glanced down at her sleeves and stopped. There were black smudges where his big hairy mitts had grabbed her.

She remembered the filth on Dalton's shirt and trousers, and the coal dust in the tunnel in the boiler room where he'd nearly caught her. Swirling black dust, like in her dream last night. Davy's smiling face seemed to float before her. This is a dusty business, he'd said.

Everything came together at once and it hit her like a rogue wave. The coal bunkers! It had been there in front of her all the time, black dirty coal dust pointing the way to her golden horse. She was sure of it.

Scrambling back to the stairs, Ailish raced down flight after flight to the lowest deck on the ship. She came to the weighty door that led to the giant boilers and shouldered her way through. The noise was deafening as steam escaped in boiling jets and furnaces roared with a fiery fury.

Ahead, she saw the tunnel through the coal bunkers. Her footfalls echoed in the confined space as she ran through the cold iron passage.

Once on the other side she looked around. She was in a long narrow anteroom. Dalton had been in a hurry, he might not have covered his tracks well. She inspected the grimy room. The walls were covered in a thick coating of soot, and everywhere, the choking dust filled the air, swirling in black eddies and settling like Spanish lace.

She looked down at the floor and smiled. A pair of large boot prints was clearly visible in the telltale dust. They led into a darkened recess at the rear of the room. Ailish followed the trail to a sea chest, ancient and weathered with a rusty padlock securing the lid. It was exactly the place to hide a plundered pirate treasure.

And now to get into the thing. Feeling the edge of the sea locker, she found what she needed. The seams were held with thin pieces of wire, exactly what the magician ordered. She picked at the frayed edge and pulled a piece of the wire free. Wiggling her magic key in the lock, she repeated the spell that went along with her trick. With a snap, the old lock sprang open.

"Thank you, Manfred the Magnificent!" Hoisting the lid, Ailish peered inside. A lump closed her throat as she looked down into the bottom of the box.

There was her da's orange striped vest tied into a loose bundle. She lifted it out and brought the cloth close to her face, inhaling the familiar scent. He'd be so glad to get it back. It was the last thing her mother had made for him and Ailish knew how much he cherished it.

Unfolding the vest, she whooped in delight. The shining gold horse winked back at her with its brilliant diamond eyes. "Hello again! I've been looking for you," she laughed. "Come on, my beauty, you're going home."

Wrapping the statue back up in the vest, Ailish carefully planned what to do next. A lot depended on timing, and even more on faith.

16

DEAL WITH A DEVIL

WITH HER DA'S HELPFUL ADVICE RINGING IN HER EARS, Ailish made one quick stop before racing to the machinery storage hold. Dalton was there with Paddy and from the tone of his voice, he sounded smug and very pleased with himself. She eased her way silently through the puzzle of boxes strewn about and listened in.

"You need to get out of the sun more, Whelan. You're addled in the brain," he tapped his own huge head. "My property is exactly where it should be and as for you… your time is up. No more waiting for you to come to your senses. With all that's been going on, you'll be lucky to make it back to port once I show the captain and crew that picture. I doubt there's a brig on any ship that could save you after my lads get the mob going. And when you've gone to your reward," he snorted what Ailish took to be the robber's version of a laugh, "I'll make sure that money you have locked in the ship's safe goes to a good home."

She'd heard enough. Taking a deep breath, Ailish stepped out from the shadows.

"I'd think twice about that, Mr. Dalton."

Dalton's face first looked surprised, then furious. "I knew you were up to no good, you little sneak." He took a menacing step toward her. "I should have made sure you were finished the night of the storm."

Paddy stepped between Ailish and Dalton. "Perhaps you'd best hear the lad out." He raised an eyebrow at Ailish. "Is it still lad we be calling you, or would you prefer your proper title?"

Dalton hesitated. "What gibberish is this?"

Ailish drew herself up with all the dignity she inherited from her proud parents. "My name is Ailish O'Connor and you stole the golden horse from my father. He offered you hospitality and you repaid his kindness by beating him unconscious in our home and then robbing him. I've come to take my property back."

Dalton's two deputies had been listening and now exchanged a look. Robbing a man who offered you the warmth of his own hearth was the mark of the lowest of men.

Recognition registered in Dalton's eyes as he finally placed her, but confronted with the truth in such a straightforward manner, he tried to bluster his way through. "I don't know what you're going on about," he sputtered, but everyone heard the lie in this.

Ailish could see him trying to figure a way out of this hole. He stared at her with cold, dead eyes. With a shudder, she edged closer to Paddy before going on.

"You've led me a merry chase and treated me very poorly, Mr. Dalton, but this morning, *in the coal hold*, I found my reward right where you'd hidden it." She tipped her head with a hint of cockiness. "I want to thank you for taking me straight to it."

Dalton's face again flared red and this time she truly hoped he would burst.

"A thief and a sneak! Where is it?" he raged, lunging toward her.

Ailish stumbled back. "Did you think I'd bring the statue with me and risk you and your thugs taking it by force? It's somewhere you'll never find it. This ship has a thousand places to hide a poor man's meagre treasure." Again, the sailors' eyes darted a look at each other. "I could leave it at that, but I'm here to offer you a deal..." She let her words hang in the air and Dalton snatched at them.

"What kind of deal?" he asked cautiously.

"It's not only me you've been giving troubles, but my friend Paddy here. You've got him standing on the gallows and you're holding the rope!" Despite the anger she felt, she kept her voice calm as she went on. "I want the picture showing Paddy with the leaders of the Fenians and I want your word that you will stop pointing the finger of guilt at him. We both know he's not a Fenian, Mr. Dalton."

The corners of the big man's mouth lifted briefly, like a sail in a weak wind. "Oh, aye, I know it, but that won't matter when the mob gets the scent of blood. Idiots like these are easily led." He jerked his head in the direction of his two companions.

Paddy's curled fists were at the ready. "You are truly despicable and if it were my future alone, I'd take my chances, but this is about my family too. And it isn't a fair fight, is it? You've poisoned the crew against me."

Ailish was afraid the two men would come to blows if she didn't do something quickly. She stepped toward Dalton. "In exchange for the picture and your help smoothing things for Paddy, I will give you my golden horse."

At the mention of the statue, the crew chief's eyes burned with greed. He looked at her slyly. "That filly is worth a fortune. I'd say trading the life of one worthless Irishman for that horse gives me the better deal." He fumbled in his vest and withdrew the incriminating photograph. "And I'll make sure the captain knows Whelan had nothing to do with the sabotage."

"You both heard him agree to the deal," she said, looking from one enforcer to the other. Their heads bobbed agreement.

Ailish reached for the photograph, but Dalton held it back. "Not so fast, O'Connor! Where's my golden horse?" A gob of spittle dribbled down his chin.

"It's topside. Come with me and I'll give it to you."

Waiting while Dalton folded the picture into a small square and put it in his vest pocket, she prayed this would work out the way it had in her dream.

When they reached the deck, Ailish felt as if she was

at the head of a parade as they marched down Oxford Street. It must have been a sight – O'Connor the cabin boy, followed by Rufus Dalton the crew chief, then Paddy Whelan, accused Fenian, and finally, two hulking sailors spoiling for a fight.

When they drew abreast of the telegraph testing caboose, Ailish stopped and looked around as though gauging her audience. "Wait here," she instructed, then ducked behind the blackout curtain.

Seconds later she emerged carrying the priceless horse. As her followers watched, she raised it high above her head so that the sunlight glinted off its golden skin in a dazzling display. The two henchmen were stunned. "This is what your boss stole from my da. He took an honest man's future."

Rufus looked around quickly to see if anyone was watching. "Are you crazy? Hide that away, you fool!"

Ailish turned the statue so that its diamond eyes glittered and the rubies sparked like fire in the sun. She could see the effect this was having on Dalton. He looked like one of the audience who assisted Manfred the Magnificent with his hypnosis act.

"The picture, give it to Paddy," she instructed Dalton.

He obligingly took the folded paper out of a pocket in his dirty work trousers. "Choke on it, Whelan," he growled as he threw it at Paddy.

With a sigh of regret, Ailish placed the beautiful little horse in Rufus Dalton's huge palm. His thick fingers curled around the delicate figurine as he squeezed it in his meaty fist.

Ailish felt a pang, but it had been worth it. She nodded at the picture. "Tear that thing into a million pieces, Paddy."

Keeping his eyes on Dalton, Paddy ripped the incriminating paper into a shower of confetti, then tossed it into the air off the starboard rail. The wind caught the fragments and sent them spinning and whirling up and away like startled birds.

Ailish felt as though a weight had been lifted off her and she knew she had done the right thing. She smiled at Paddy. "Now you won't have to be looking over your shoulder to make sure no one's coming for you."

"Oh, my girl, the price was too steep." Paddy looked stricken.

"A friend is worth more than all the gold in the world." She smiled reassuringly.

Dalton's guttural laugh interrupted her.

"You Irish really are country bumpkins. You can say I stole the horse from you, but my boys here will swear it's mine. And as for the picture, did you think I'd give it over just like that?" He snapped his fat, sausage fingers. "You'll never walk off this ship, Whelan. Fenian traitors get what they deserve and delivering a Fenian who is also a saboteur should be worth a reward or a promotion, maybe both to Captain Anderson."

He reached into the pocket of his vest and withdrew

a folded square of paper, then opened it. "See anyone you recognize?"

It was the picture from the newspaper. He had given them a fake! The swine had no intentions of keeping his end of the bargain. The dummy picture was proof that he still planned to turn Paddy over to the mob.

Ailish could trace her Irish ancestry back a hundred generations and at this moment, every one of those ancestors screamed for her to get Rufus Dalton.

"Thank you for making this so easy." Reaching inside her threadbare shirt, she withdrew the shiny whistle she'd found in the Family Saloon and blew on it with all her might. The noise echoed up and down the deck like a banshee's wail.

Heads turned and immediately, a crowd formed around the group. Captain Anderson along with Cyrus Field and Samuel Canning emerged from the telegraph testing caboose.

"What in thunder is going on here, Mr. Dalton?" the captain asked tersely.

Ailish stepped forward. "Mr. Dalton is returning my property to me, Captain. That statue is mine."

Everyone, including Rufus Dalton looked down at the figurine. The little horse glowed in the sun.

"This," he sputtered, holding it up as though surprised to find it in his hand, "...why, this is mine. The little thief stole it from me and now he's trying to say it was his." Then he seemed to remember something that needed to be shared. "Why he's not even a boy, Captain, this here is a girl masquerading. It seems this one is not only a thief but a liar."

All those around were now listening closely and Ailish could hear mutterings as they stared. The Captain simply appraised her as if trying to see for himself if this was true.

She was in a corner and decided *in for a penny, in for a pound.* She'd given Dalton one last chance to get out of this unscathed, but he had lit the fuse, now she would fire the cannon.

"That's correct sir. My name is Ailish O'Connor, and I am a girl." She felt her face blush as she smoothed back a chunk of her shorn locks. "But I had no choice in what I've done. Rufus Dalton stole that golden horse from my father and I had to get it from him. Davy said the only way you'd let me stay aboard was if I became a cabin boy, so I did. I tricked Dalton into leading me to the horse then made a bargain with him that if he stopped trying to make everyone believe Paddy was a Fenian, which is a lie, I'd give it back. But Mr. Dalton reneged on our deal and I had no choice but to bring it to your attention."

Captain Anderson harrumphed. "Indeed, I'd say that shrill of yours has everyone's attention, *Miss* O'Connor."

Ailish saw the loathing in Dalton's eyes, but there was something else waiting behind his hooded lids, a faltering, like the moment after a tree has been sawed through, but before it falls.

"That's all nonsense, Captain," he blustered. "Where would an Irish street urchin get a valuable trinket like this? I bought it from a sailor in Sheerness and am taking it home to my wife in Liverpool. She's expecting our tenth bairn and I wanted to give her something pretty."

Ailish swallowed and crossed her fingers in the faint hope that her brazen plan would succeed. She could see the hesitation in the captain's eyes. He was wavering and she had to stop Dalton's momentum.

"I can prove the statue is mine!" she hastily blurted. "I need only one minute, Captain." Without waiting, she darted into the blacked out telegraph room, leaving a murmur of voices in her wake.

The darkness enveloped her and she stopped to give her eyes a second to adjust. She'd never been one for risks, but she'd taken one now. She'd gambled everything on the power of the mighty transatlantic cable. It was to be a miracle of communication and she prayed it would live up to its expectations.

"Joe, did it work?" she asked into the silence.

"As well as if the great man were sitting in this room," her operator friend replied with a laugh.

He gave her a note and she thanked all the saints for their help as she stepped back outside.

Ailish brandished the piece of paper as though she were Joan of Arc and it her victorious sword. "I have a telegram dated today, August 2, 1865, received here on the *Great Eastern* from Sir Peter Fitzgerald, the Knight of

Kerry, in Ireland testifying that he saw the bill of sale for that statue and that my father, Michael O'Connor, is the rightful owner." Her voice was clear and carried across the crowded deck as she passed the paper to the captain, trying to hide the trembling in her fingers. She blessed her da for bragging to Uncle Peter and showing him the proof that they owned the magnificent horse.

Captain Anderson read the telegram and gave it to Cyrus Field.

He read it, and then smiled wryly at Ailish. "Nicely played, young lady. I may have something to add to your victory." With a bow, he left the gathered group, his Inverness cape swaying jauntily, and then he disappeared into the cable tank.

"Mr. Dalton, please return Miss O'Connor's property to her!" The weighty authority in the captain's voice could not be denied.

As though he were surrendering his first born child, Rufus Dalton reluctantly returned the precious statue to Ailish. "You may have won this one O'Connor, but Whelan's forfeit."

And with that, he turned his venomous gaze on Paddy and addressed the crowd. "As a good Englishman, I feel there's something Captain Anderson should know. I have proof that Paddy Whelan is a Fenian traitor!" Triumphantly, he drew out the infamous picture. "Here is a photograph in the London Illustrated News of him consorting with the Fenian leaders!"

Paddy spoke up in his own defence. "Captain Anderson, that is not true. I was at that meeting to hear what they had to say and that is all. I'm not a Fenian. You've got to believe me."

The captain took the picture and examined it.

At that moment, Dalton's two thugs glanced at each other and nodded then one stepped forward.

"We want to say something, Cap'n. We heard Mr. Dalton say he knew Paddy, I mean, Mr. Whelan, was no Fenian. He was blackmailing him, sir. Planning on inciting a riot, he was, so Paddy would be killed and he could steal the poor fellow's money."

Thug Number Two then added his piece. "And we can vouch for O'Connor's owning that horse too. We should have said something earlier, but we only recently realized what kind of a crew chief and what kind of a man Dalton really is." With a last scornful look at their former boss, the two sailors retreated into the crowd.

Captain Anderson's steely gaze was riveted on Rufus Dalton, and his disgust at the dirty tactics used was there for all to see. Slowly, he held up the picture for the crowd.

"Gentlemen, as it happens, I was at this same meeting! If you look in the background, you can see me standing with a group of colleagues, including Sir Geoffrey Thornton, a distinguished Member of Parliament and Clyde Swinton-Jones, Earl of Hardwickshire. This picture means nothing."

Ailish blinked in amazement then looked at Paddy

who shook his head ruefully.

"All I had to do was stand up to this bully and trust in the truth! Captain, I want you to know that O'Connor here," he corrected himself, "I mean Miss O'Connor, is a hardworking, honest member of the crew. She is blameless in all this, sir, and was only trying to do what was right by her father and by me. She is a loyal friend."

"At ease, Mr. Whelan. I think there is enough evidence to assure Mr. Dalton a lengthy stay in the brig. I will compile a list of charges, and then when I'm through with him, I shall turn him over to the civilian authorities." He looked meaningfully at Dalton. "We shall give Mr. O'Connor the opportunity to press charges."

Ailish felt like singing. She had her wonderful horse and Paddy was safe. They were both going to have a bright and wonderful future. Not a bad day's work, she congratulated herself and all before ten o'clock in the morning!

Suddenly, a sound that chilled the bone echoed across the quiet deck.

It was the mournful dirge of the alarm gong!

17

SABOTAGE UNCOVERED

.-- .... .- -   ... .- -.. --- .- --. .- -..   - ..... -.. .- .- -... .-..

W**ITH AN ORGANISED FRENZY, EVERYONE ON DECK MOVED**
at once. Captain Anderson, issuing orders as he went,
strode purposefully toward the bridge to supervise the
retrieval of the cable. Men ran down Oxford Street to
stop the clanking machinery, others went to the tank
access, while still more moved to their assigned stations in
preparation for cutting and transferring the weighty
length of wire to the bow. Paddy was about to go assist
with the dangerous job of splicing when a shout rang out.

"Wait! Look here!" Cyrus Field, emerging from the
dark recesses of the cable tank, called in a loud voice
which carried over the raucous noise on deck. Everyone
stopped, looking to the American for an explanation. He
caught Ailish's eye and with a nod went on. "I have solved
the mystery of the cable faults!"

Ailish wondered if she'd heard correctly. Mr. Field
had found the villain causing the troubles!

All around her, others were reacting the same way.
His words acted like a magnet as men crowded to see

what had been discovered. Finally, the truth would be known and the real saboteur unmasked!

The shouting soon brought Samuel Canning and Professor Thomson on deck. They joined the throng that had gathered to listen. Even the gong was still as the entire ship waited for the perpetrator to be named.

Mr. Field waved them all to silence. "This, gentlemen, is a day to remember. The grievous damage done to the cable has been explained. I have our culprit!" He held up a small piece of wire that looked exactly like the others that had been stabbed through the heart of the cable. "This is what caused the faults!"

He went on, silencing the murmurs. "This is a shard of the iron sheathing that is wrapped around the cable to protect it from the ravages of its ocean home. Fragments of this outer casing broke off when the cable was being stored in the tanks, and the weight of the coils, piled one on top of the other, drove the deadly sliver into the wire. I discovered several of these and know it was the cable itself that did the damage and not any man." He glanced meaningfully at Paddy.

Paddy, standing next to Ailish, nodded. "This will lay to rest any lingering doubts about me the lads may have had."

Ailish could practically feel him relax.

Samuel Canning, who was in charge of the cable-laying, stepped forward. "The loss of signal is not one hundred percent this time, but after discussing the situation, we have decided we still need to repair the fault to ensure the strongest signal possible. We shall continue the splicing with all haste."

"Aye, and that means lots of hard work," Paddy said. "I'd best get at it." He gave her a tip of his cap and moved off.

As the crowd dispersed, Ailish could hear men saying they had known all along it wasn't Paddy Whelan and that he was a good Irishman.

Ailish decided the hearts of men were more changeable than the winds at sea.

During Mr. Field's revelation, Ailish had stood clutching the small bejewelled horse. She knew there was nothing she could do to aid the cable repair but stay out of the way and fetch gallons of hot coffee to the men as they laboured to fix the dead line.

Deciding she would not tempt fate or the honesty of the rest of the crew now that the news of her fabulous horse was sure to have spread, she stopped at the purser's office to have her treasure locked up next to Paddy's in the ship's safe, then she went to the machinery storage hold to tell Davy what had happened.

— - • — —

DAVY, SITTING ON HIS BOX, SMILED BROADLY WHEN HE saw her. "Tell me all about your adventures. I'm in need of hearing something other than the clang of that accursed hammer of Charlie's."

Ailish settled opposite him and recounted the entire tale, from beginning to end, then retold him about the cable itself proving Paddy innocent because she liked the sound of the words as she spoke them. *Innocent. Not a Fenian.* They were all great words.

She could tell Davy truly enjoyed her company and her story, which she drew out with as much detail as possible. "So you see, everything is working fantastically well. My da and I will soon be owning our own fishing boat and real house in our new home in Newfoundland and Paddy will take his money to his family so they will be safe." She stood up and stretched. "And now, I'd best be going topside to see if there's anything I can do."

"Don't go yet!" Davy pleaded. "You've only just arrived."

Although they both knew this to be untrue, something in his voice tugged at her. He sounded so lonely. There were five hundred men aboard and even working the dreadful hours he did, there was time to socialize; still, she remembered how she never saw him anywhere but here. A pleasant shiver danced down her spine, making it tingle. She sucked in her breath at the unexpected sensation.

She would like to have stayed, but after all that had happened on this voyage, she felt like a member of the crew and as a member of the crew, she wanted to help. Captain Anderson had been very good to her. He had not so much as given her a lecture for all her deception and she wanted to repay his loyalty in kind.

"I'll be back later to let you know how the cable repair fares." Her face lit up with an idea. "Maybe we can go to the mess and eat together. Surely Charlie will let you have an hour off this once. We have to celebrate how well everything turned out, not to mention my changing back into a girl, although what my da will say when he sees my hair is still uncharted waters, probably pretty choppy waters at that."

"You won't forget me will you, Ails?" Davy asked unexpectedly. His voice was barely more than a sigh.

"Don't be daft!" she laughed. "How could I ever forget you?"

Davy's spirit seemed to lift as he smiled and waved when she left.

— - • — —

IT WAS NEAR NOON AND AILISH DECIDED LUNCH FOR ALL was called for. She went to the galley and Henry loaded her up with a variety of hearty fare. Her offering was so successful, she spent the next hour running back and forth, bringing food to the tireless crew.

Finally, she was ready for a bite herself, and scanned the bedlam looking for Paddy. Moving down Oxford Street, she found him on a small platform working the brake above the wheel reeling in the cable. "You better eat now, Mr. Whelan. On this ship, one never knows what calamity awaits over the next wave."

Paddy smiled wryly. "Truer words were never spoken, O'Connor."

Ailish was going to correct him, but then realized that she liked the name. She'd changed since coming aboard the *Great Eastern*. She had gained a world of confidence and knew so much more than that silly stowaway who'd boarded two weeks ago.

"O'Connor, are you listening?" Paddy teased, bringing her attention back from her woolgathering. "I was saying we're now only 600 miles from Newfoundland and that means we're trailing 1,186 miles of cable! A mighty weight dragging at us for sure, which is why they put me on the brake." His eyes crinkled at the corners. "It turns out, I'm the best darn brakeman aboard and we don't want to snap our delicate thread."

"Well, even the best darn brakeman aboard needs to eat."

With a nod to his replacement, Paddy followed the cabin boy.

They sat near the edge of the deck, away from the noisy machinery to eat their food. The sun was warm, the ocean tranquil and if it weren't for the current crisis, Ailish might have thought it the perfect day. They polished off their Cornish pasties, tarts and coffee then sat in companionable silence.

At that precise moment a terrific crack rang out.

Like a live thing escaping from captivity, the cable flew through the brake unchecked, then leapt out over the waiting sea and dove beneath the waves.

"Oh no!" Ailish gasped in astonishment. "It's gone! The transatlantic cable is lost!"

Paddy sprang to his feet and ran to the bow. When he returned to Ailish, he confirmed it: the cable had disappeared below, leaving not a ripple. All the hopes and dreams of so many men were now resting three miles below them on the silty floor of the Atlantic Ocean.

18

FISHING OFF THE
GRAND BANKS

.-- ....- .-.. .-- .-.- ... - ..... .-- ...-.. .-. --- .-... ... - --- .-- . -..

SOON THE WHOLE CREW WAS ASSEMBLED, EVERYONE speculating on what had happened. Captain Anderson came on deck and looked like he'd aged ten years. The tumult stilled as the crew waited to hear his words.

"At some point, the ship floated over the cable, so that it was rubbing against the hull as it was pulled in. This weakened the cable, and once the damaged section went into the machinery, the strain was too much and it snapped."

He paused, and took a deep breath, as if to steady himself. "We've had a setback and are now trying to decide what to do. The cable is at a great depth and we are indeed in dire straights."

With the captain were the usual gentlemen and none appeared to be holding out any hope that this expedition could be salvaged. They talked among themselves, but from the amount of head shaking, it didn't seem like a solution was going to be presented.

Paddy looked at Ailish soberly, the disappointment evident on his face. "This is the end of the line, lass. We're sure to return to Ireland with our tail between our legs now."

Ailish didn't like the thought of quitting, not after how hard everyone had worked. A crazy, if not desperate, idea came to her. "Couldn't we *fish* for the cable, Paddy?" She could tell from his expression that he did not understand what she was getting at. "You know, throw a giant hook into the water, let it drop to the bottom, then trawl for the cable, like they do cod in Newfoundland."

His tone was sceptical. "It's a long way down. We'd need miles of line and there isn't that much on the ship."

A detail forgotten from weeks ago bobbed to the surface of her mind. "When I first came aboard, I was in a small room at the back of the machinery storage hold and in it were rolls and rolls of wire rope. That would work wonderfully for our fishing line. All we have to find is the hook!"

Paddy's excitement mounted as he realized what this could mean. "How much of this wire did you see?"

She squeezed her eyes shut trying to remember. "Loads! Miles of the stuff."

"We could lower a grappling hook and drag the ocean floor until we catch the cable, then haul it up and splice it together." He clapped her joyfully on the back, nearly sending her flying in his enthusiasm. "Well done, O'Connor! Come on, we'll go propose your solution to the captain."

Together, they hurried to Captain Anderson with the plan.

His expression went from desperation to hope as he listened. And then a slow smile spread from ear to ear. "By Jove, O'Connor, this could work! We'll fish that cable right out of the sea!"

The captain immediately summoned Samuel Canning and Cyrus Field to tell them of the bold idea. The gloomy atmosphere on board lifted. There was hope the transatlantic cable could be saved.

As the *Great Eastern* headed south, all was made ready. The line was brought up from the storage room and found to be five miles long, divided into hundred-fathom lengths. Paddy voiced concern that it was not continuous.

"There's naught for it, lads, we'll have to shackle the sections together. Pay particular attention to the joins as this is going to be like lifting an elephant with a shoestring." Paddy and the crew set to work joining the sections.

When Samuel Canning heard Paddy was in need of a grappling hook, he amazed everyone by producing a box containing several that were perfect for the job.

Finally all was ready and at three in the afternoon, the fishing expedition for the lost transatlantic cable began. After two hours, the constant whirring of the wheels and pulleys letting out the line suddenly stopped. All hands were immediately at their stations, ready to start dragging for the cable.

Ailish had refused to leave the deck, and her interest

was rewarded when a flicker of action high above the deck caught her attention. "What's happening up there?"

Paddy, standing beside her, shaded his eyes and gazed upward. "Captain Anderson doesn't want to risk snaring the line in the paddlewheels or screw. So, O'Connor, you are about to behold a spectacle few have seen, the *Great Eastern* under sail. We'll be loosing only four of her tops'ls as we need to move ahead dead slow."

As she watched, the sails billowed out, filling the rigging with vast sheets of snow-white canvas to harness the wind. Immediately, the ship was turned into a nautical fantasy as sailors scampered up and down ropes and indecipherable orders were shouted in a language known only to those of the sea. Paddy shooed her toward the hatchway that led belowdecks. "It could take hours or even days to find it. Remember, we're looking for something an inch across, three miles under the ocean. Get some rest."

Exhausted, Ailish reluctantly agreed. "You promise you'll call me if you find it?"

He patted her on the shoulder. "I'll fetch you the minute we hook our prize."

— - • — —

AT SIX O'CLOCK THE NEXT MORNING, AILISH WAS IN THE mess hall bolting down her bowl of porridge, when Paddy sat at her table. She looked up and saw the excitement in his eyes.

"We've caught it?" she asked expectantly.

"That we have. Exactly where Captain Anderson's sextant reading from yesterday said it would be."

Ailish pushed the bowl away and jumped up. "I'm done, let's go, man!"

On deck, they went straight to the bow and the machinery that was poised to begin the huge task of retrieving the miles of cable. Ailish watched from a safe distance as the engine powering the winch chugged to life. She could see Paddy carefully gauging the strain and speed and she remembered his worry about the cobbled sections that had been so painstakingly joined together.

It seemed the entire ship was holding its breath waiting as the whirr of the wheel brought more and more of their fishing line to the surface. Ailish felt the tension of the men.

Without warning, there was a loud snap as one of the shackles broke apart, sending the broken wire whizzing through the wheel as it again tried to return to the sea.

The end of the wire thrashed and flailed about the deck, striking like an iron sea serpent with lethal force, slashing all in its path. It shredded skin and smashed bones, tearing to pieces the helpless men who scrambled to escape. Blood splattered Ailish's shirt as she ducked behind the shelter of a cannon.

With lightning speed, Paddy reached out and clamped on the brake, leaning on it as he tried with all his might to stop the desperate escape attempt of the demon wire. With a growl of metal and a scream of complaining wheels, the brake grabbed hold and the broken wire shuddered and dropped to the deck, lifeless once more.

A cheer went up, and Paddy brought out his tools then began calmly affixing a new shackle before starting the engine again and freeing the brake. Ailish was going to clap and whistle too, but then noticed her bloody shirt and saw the unconscious sailors, their ruined bodies like rag dolls, being taken below.

With this sobering start, everyone knew they were in for a mighty battle. The cable continued to fight them as it tried to return to its watery home. When the shackles gave way again, the crew was unable to stop it in time and they had to begin fishing once more.

And, as every man aboard stood united in the goal of completing their task, whatever it took, a new saboteur raised her head: mother nature.

Helplessly, they watched as a dense fog rolled in, shrouding the ship and calling a halt to their endeavours. The silvery grey mist refused to abate, and as the days past, the crew had no choice but to wait.

Ailish spent much of the time in the hold talking to Davy, who knew an incredible amount about the construction of the *Great Eastern.* He told her stories of the men who built the ship and the trials that had to be overcome when constructing a vessel larger and more advanced than anything that had ever floated. His vivid detail and minute descriptions made her feel as though she were there, watching the *Great Eastern* rise plate by plate and bolt by bolt. Since he was not much older than she, Davy must have heard all these fabulous tales from his father and had listened very closely indeed to remember so much.

The morning of the fifth day, a hopeful glimmer of sunlight poked through the thick fog and everyone's spirits brightened. Paddy and the crew eagerly took their stations, lowering the fishing wire and watching for the telltale strain that would signal they'd caught the cable.

"We've hooked it!" Paddy at last sang out, but this time, no cheer went up. Instead, everyone bent to their task. The hours slowly passed as Ailish watched the men steadily and very cautiously haul in the cable.

Continuing her vigil that evening, she sat perched on top of the cannon, enjoying the crisp salt air and clear starry night. She wished her da was with her, having a pipe and a mug so they could once again talk, content in each other's company. She now looked at her world differently and it made her even more proud of her father. He was not the richest man, true, but he was ingenious at keeping their little caravan rolling and even if they ate potatoes more than she liked, Ailish knew he always did his best and that he loved her. What more could a daughter ask for?

— – • – —

THE NEXT DAY, MOTHER NATURE ONCE MORE DISPLAYED her fearsome power. The crew was finishing their last preparations to drop the line, after having gained, then lost the cable one more time earlier that morning. In dismay, the men watched as an ominous pillar of black thunderheads rose on the horizon.

"We're in for a blow, lads!" Paddy said, trying to hide his disappointment. "We'd best lower a buoy to mark our spot. I have a feeling this will get rough."

It was indeed bad luck and another serious setback. But as Ailish looked around at the crew, she saw no signs of defeat. Instead, everyone busied themselves preparing for the storm to come. How could these sailors keep going in the face of all that had happened? She saw that it wasn't only the *Great Eastern* that was made of iron, but everyone who sailed aboard her.

The gale hit with pounding waves and hurricane winds. The mighty ship rolled and wallowed as she stoically endured all the sea threw at her. The battle never let up and as Ailish sat huddled in her big bed listening to the howling of the storm, she was thankful that Davy and Charlie had done such a good job of keeping the *Great Eastern* shipshape.

Finally, dawn broke and with it the tempest abated. With the sun came renewed hope as the men doggedly set to work preparing the grapnel for its long descent.

When Ailish went on deck, she felt that today would be an extra important one.

"Are you a betting man, Mr. Whelan?" she asked, handing Paddy one of the steaming cups of coffee she'd brought with her from the galley. "I'll wager we finish the job this try."

"I'm worried saying it out loud will jinx it, O'Connor. Before I face that engine again, let me finish my mug in peace." He motioned her to the ship's rail and together, they watched the sun scribing its arc over the silky water. Again, she was struck with the wonder of the sea, the indomitable power hiding beneath that tranquil surface.

"You're right about one thing, lass, today is the day."

Something in his tone alerted her. "Yes…" She drew out the word. "Today we bring up the cable and continue our journey to Heart's Content. By tonight, we'll be steaming west."

He turned to her, mouth set firmly. "I don't think you understand. We've used every scrap of wire, hemp rope and manila line we have aboard. There is no more."

Her face fell as the full meaning of his words became clear. "So this is the last chance. If the grappling line breaks again and the wire sinks to the ocean bottom, we'll have no choice but to go back to Ireland."

He nodded. "One way or another, O'Connor, today is the day."

She knew all hands had said a silent prayer as the last of the cobbled wire was cast into the ocean, then everyone waited to see if they could hook their elusive fish.

Two hours later, Paddy waved and this time, the men did cheer. "We've got it!" He fired up the engine and working levers and gears, set the machine rattling and banging as it brought up the prize.

Tension had never been higher. Ailish felt she could squeeze it in her fist and wring out the sweat. All day, the engine toiled as fathom after fathom of wire was reeled back in. There was not a breath of breeze, as though the very air around them knew the import of this day. Captain Anderson strode up and down Oxford Street, looking severe, and Ailish thought he was trying to make the cable appear through sheer force of will.

The first hundred-fathom join came up with no problem, then the next, and the next. Mutterings took on a hopeful tone. The next hundred was hauled aboard and the one after that and still the wire held.

Ailish wanted to get closer, to offer a few words of encouragement to Paddy, but she knew he was so focused on his job, that any distraction would not be welcome.

It was evening and the eighth join had been safely pulled up when Ailish saw something odd about the line. It looked somehow thinner than the previous sections, as though it were stretched to its limit.

Before she could say a word, the wire gave way, flew through the capstan and was gone, quicker than the gasp that escaped Ailish's lips.

No anguished cry arose from the crew. No frantic scrambling to prepare another attempt. Everything they had worked for so tirelessly was swallowed in one bite by the relentless ocean, leaving not a ripple on the surface.

They were defeated.

19

THE FUTURE IS WAITING

THE MOOD WAS SOMBER AS THE CREW SHUT OFF THE machines and put away their tools. Ailish ran to Paddy. "It's really over, then?"

"Aye, lass. This is the end of it." His voice was strained and despair written plainly on his face. Wiping his hands with a rag, he leaned against one of the cannon. Ailish noticed a deep gash scored the barrel from the deadly encounter with the lethal wire. "I'm looking on the bright side, small though it may be. My family may have to wait a little longer for their money, but at least they'll get it and me, safe and sound."

"And the O'Connors will be the ones appearing in the pages of the *Irish Times* as newly wealthy emigrants to Newfoundland." She grinned self-consciously up at him. "It was quite the adventure, wasn't it?"

"Like no other – and I don't just mean the laying of the transatlantic cable. We made a fine pair, Miss O'Connor. Two Irishmen on a mission."

"Two Irish *persons*," she corrected, "and I wholeheartedly agree, Mr. Whelan!" Unexpectedly, a lump seemed to form in her throat. "Paddy, it's been a privilege being here on the *Great Eastern* and to see everyone working together to make this venture a success. This isn't the end. Men like Cyrus Field and Mr. Canning, not to mention Professor Thompson, will never let the dream die. The future is waiting. I know the transatlantic cable will work; that one day, ghost messages will be flying thick and fast all over the world. I get a tingly feeling when I think about it and my tingly feelings are never wrong."

They exchanged a look and she knew no more words were necessary. They were friends and always would be, no matter the time or tides that lay ahead.

— – • — —

PADDY LEFT TO REJOIN THE MEN AND AILISH CONTINUED to watch the activities on deck. She wondered what would happen next. Her answer came through the deck under her feet as she felt the *Great Eastern's* engines begin to pound. Slowly the bow of the ship swung eastward as Captain Anderson, reacting swiftly to this last disaster, started their long journey home.

Disappointment, weariness and a terrible sadness overtook Ailish. Not wanting her crewmates to see her so dejected, she silently slipped below to her quarters. "Stop being such a baby," she chided herself, but it was no use. She couldn't stem the sudden flood of tears and she wept into her pillow, not for herself, but for all the stalwart crew who had tried so hard and given so much. Her eyes, red and swollen, grew heavy and she fell into a restless sleep, filled with strange dreams.

Davy Jones moved languorously through all of them and each time she saw him, he grew more transparent, becoming a will-o-the-wisp, a breath of air on a frosty morning. And always, in her dreamscapes, he was walking by her side but just out of reach.

The minute Ailish awoke she went in search of her friend. She hadn't meant to nap and knew he would be desperate for news. As she made her way down to the storage hold, she was unable to set aside the feeling that there was something she couldn't quite grasp, something cloudy and intangible like the mist in her dreams.

It was a relief to see Davy on his usual crate. His face told her he already knew the fate of the cable.

"We're bound for Ireland now," she said with a half-hearted smile. "And I'll be showing my da this wretched hair."

"It's growing on me." Davy tipped his head. "Or maybe I should say it's growing on you. I'll bet he'll be that glad to see you, he won't notice the stylish new bob."

That's what she loved about him. Davy could always make her feel better, no matter what. "I'm guessing that means we'll be parting ways soon." She had to force the words out as they seemed to stick.

"Aye, my girl, that it does."

She went on haltingly. "I want to thank you again for,

for...being such a good friend. I couldn't have made it without you."

The look he gave her was filled with warmth. "No, Ails, it's the other way around. I couldn't have made it without you! It's been a long time since I had anyone to talk to. You have no idea how much I'll miss you."

Ailish thought of all they'd been through. Davy had been getting her out of trouble from the first time she set foot on the deck plates of his ship and soon, they would be separated forever. It was strange how in such a short time, she'd become so close to this bash boy that the thought of leaving him behind was impossible.

She didn't want to say goodbye. "Davy, why don't you come with me when we reach Valentia? Once my da sells the wonderful horse, there will be more than enough money to give all of us a new start." It was insane, yet in her heart, this is what she truly wanted and she was desperate now. "You could come to Newfoundland with us. They have lots of boats there. Why, a lad who knows the workings of ships as much as you do would be able to find employment in no time..."

But Davy was slowly shaking his head. The sadness on his face tore at her and she knew what he was going to say.

"That's a fine dream, lass, but no. Even if there was a way for me to go with you, my place is here on my ship." He smiled at her, but the smile never reached his remarkable eyes. "Besides, who'd look after that big galoot Charlie? He'd be lost without me. We're as much a part of the *Great Eastern* as the iron plates and rivets holding her together."

His voice was as soft as a sea breeze and Ailish felt an odd prickling sensation, like when your foot goes to sleep. Then waves of warmth started inside her and spread outward to her fingers and toes, the heat building from a spark to a flame. Trembling, she forced herself back under control and quenched the invisible fire.

Davy stood up. "There's Charlie calling. I'd best be getting back to work." Smiling, he gave her a roguish wink. "I can promise you this: you'll always be my favourite cabin boy." He turned to leave, then stopped and faced her. "There's an old sentiment that says as long as you keep a loved one in your heart, they are with you always. You'll always be with me, Ailish O'Connor."

He walked away and as she watched, a trick of the light made it seem as though he was growing transparent, fading, until he disappeared into the darkness.

EPILOGUE

September 8, 1866

.-- ....-- .--.-... -...-...--.--

IT HAD BEEN A YEAR SINCE THE DISASTROUS CABLE-laying attempt, but as Ailish stood once more at the bow of the *Great Eastern*, it seemed like a lifetime ago. They were anchored at Heart's Content, Newfoundland, and this time, the transatlantic cable had been successfully laid with not one mishap. The most important undertaking in the world was finally a success story, one for the history books.

Far below, Ailish could see Cyrus Field, up to his knees in the chilly bay water, as he supervised hauling the shore cable. This heavier end would be spliced to the much thinner cable they had laid and the flurry of telegraph signals would begin. She admired the friendly American. His vision led him to invest more money in this year's success and she hoped he made a million pounds and was famous forever.

As she watched, he turned and saluted, his wide grin flashing up at her. She nodded back; then hugged her father, as he kissed the top of her head. Her hair was longer again, but she didn't wear it in braids or flying wildly loose as a young girl would. She swept it up now, and it made her feel very ladylike. Her stylish Dublin clothes added to her new mystique, and her da looked a proper gentleman, too, with his tall beaver hat and long frock coat.

When she'd returned to Ireland last year, her da, healthy once more, had been overjoyed to see her. He'd thought it miraculous that she came back not only with the wonderful golden horse, but with two sheep in tow. Now, when they sat together in the evenings, he never failed to ask for another story about her time aboard the *Great Eastern*. His taste for whiskey was gone. Instead, they drank pots of the strongest tea in the world and Ailish loved it.

"This crossing was nothing like last year's," she said to Captain Anderson, who stood next to Ailish and her da.

He nodded as the corners of his mouth twitched. "Agreed. I didn't have an impudent stowaway to knock me down."

She giggled. "I turned out to be a very helpful stowaway. I took great care of Dimples and Rainbow and they will certainly love their new home."

Michael O'Connor smiled. "Thanks to that wondrous little horse, we were able to buy that fine fishing boat for me and an even grander house on the harbour for Ails. I think my daughter will make a wonderful chatelaine and we'd be proud if you'd stay with us when you're in port,

Captain Anderson."

"That would be very generous, sir. It would be a true kindness if I had a bed that didn't move with the tide." He stroked his precisely trimmed beard. "I had a piece of news you may be interested in. Rufus Dalton is enjoying a lengthy stay in Newgate Prison for a series of crimes reported, they say, by ex-members of his gang. I'm happy your treasure wasn't added to the list of stolen and lost property."

"And Paddy Whelan, have you any word of him?" Ailish asked.

"No, lass, but I'm sure that clever young man is doing fine."

Her father looked at his new watch. "It's time to go ashore, me darlin'. We'd best get our belongings."

Ailish didn't want to leave the ship, not yet. At the beginning of the crossing, she'd asked after Davy Jones, even gone looking for him – but she'd been unable to find him, and no one had seen or heard of the riveter and his bash boy. She hadn't wanted to bother the captain with it during the cable laying, but now was her last chance to find out.

"Captain Anderson, would you answer one more question?"

He nodded kindly. "Why, certainly, my dear."

"Last year, I was friends with the bash boy in the hold, but this trip, he wasn't on board. Do you know what happened to him?"

Captain Anderson looked puzzled. "I remember you mentioning something about this fellow before. You must be mistaken. There was no bash boy aboard, then or now."

She shook her head adamantly. "Mistaken? No, sir. Davy worked with a riveter on the iron plates belowdecks. Why, I talked with him there many times."

"Miss O'Connor," the captain began indulgently, "I am quite certain there was no bash boy in the hold. There hasn't been since the last plates were affixed, in 1857."

A frown creased his brow and he seemed to be recalling some forgotten fragment of information. "There is, however, a legend that has attached itself to the *Great Eastern*. It tells of a riveter and his bash boy who fell while working between the double hulls when building the ship. The calamitous noise of two hundred riveters hammering away drowned out their cries, and they were walled up alive. It is said you can hear a ghostly hammering belowdecks as they continue to pound in their phantom rivets."

Ailish felt dizzy. A long-ago memory surfaced, of Ma telling her it was possible for fey souls like them to speak to someone who had passed over, gone to the other side. She'd said it started with a numb sort of tingling that turned into a white-hot heat, like a fever were burning inside.

The last time she and Davy had spoken, she had felt that heat.

A thousand clues she'd missed at the time flooded her head. His detailed stories about the building of the *Great*

Eastern, clear as if he'd been there; his magic trick with the gaslights, and the way he'd appeared in the dark passage just when she'd needed him. And her name, she couldn't remember ever telling him, yet he knew it. His old-fashioned clothes – had she ever seen him in anything but those same faded breeches? And all the mysterious notes – on every one, the ink had blurred and faded away.

She remembered the day she'd wanted to touch him, and he'd become so angry, spouting that nonsense about Ailish thinking he wasn't good enough for her. He hadn't wanted her to touch him because he knew she *couldn't* touch him!

And in all the time she'd been with Davy, she had never seen him any place but belowdecks. The reason was now so obvious. And his answer to her – "*We're as much a part of the Great Eastern as the iron plates and rivets holding her together.*" It had been the literal truth.

Their last meeting tumbled into her mind. Her invitation for him to leave the ship and join her and Da – it had seemed crazy even at the time, so perhaps she had known, deep in her bones.

Davy Jones was a, a …

She couldn't say it.

"That is truly a tragic tale, Captain Anderson." She smiled tremulously. "If anyone asks, the riveter was named Charlie and the bash boy who died was a remarkable young man by the name of David Jones."

– – • – –

LATER, STANDING BESIDE HER DA ON THE DECK OF THE launch, Ailish looked back at the mighty vessel. It took a long time to get distance enough to see it entirely. The *Great Eastern* was a ship like no other and a true leviathan of the seas.

At last, shading her eyes against the morning sun's glare, Ailish was able to take it all in. Then she saw, high up on the catwalk, a solitary figure silhouetted against the brilliant blue sky.

The figure waved.

What had Davy said? *"I don't go on deck unless it's for someone incredible and extraordinary."*

Smiling at the compliment, she waved back as hard as she could, then watched as he faded into thin air.

Ailish slipped a hand into her pocket and curled her fingers protectively around the rusted old rivet nestled at the bottom. Tears sparkled on her lashes as she remembered his words. *As long as you keep a loved one in your heart, they are with you always.*

"You will be with me always, Davy Jones," she whispered. "You and your ghost messages."

AUTHOR'S NOTE

While speaking to students on the brilliant devices we use to chat to friends today I realized they had no idea how it all began. The marvels of communication we enjoy in the 21st century make it difficult to fathom that it wasn't always as it is now. Text messaging, e-mails, satellites and high speed Internet are built upon much humbler beginnings and Canada, especially Newfoundland, played an important role. I decided to investigate and *Ghost Messages* is the result of that snooping into the dusty past.

Ghost Messages tells of the 1865 attempt to lay the first trans-Atlantic cable which would connect the two halves of the world with instant communication. The communication wasn't digital; it wasn't fibre optics or telephone; in fact, it wasn't even a human voice. It was Morse code transmitted for 2300 nautical miles in dots and dashes along a one-inch thread composed of seven strands of fragile copper wire! (I am pleased to say I have a piece of that original wire cable, dredged up from the bottom of the ocean, and enjoy showing students when I give presentations in schools.)

At the time, a transatlantic cable was thought to be an impossibility – science fiction – but this was an age of miracles when some of the greatest men of vision and science worked together to create miracles of their own. Their names are synonymous with world-changing advances: Cyrus Field, Samuel Canning, Isambard Brunel, Daniel Gooch, William Thomson (later known as Lord Kelvin), Samuel Morse and Michael Faraday. All of these gentlemen, and many more, contributed to this project.

The *Great Eastern* was a remarkable ship – it was five times larger than any vessel built, was seven hundred feet long and utilized three methods of propulsion – sail, propeller and paddlewheel. The innovative double hull made it unsinkable and nearly indestructible, requiring the invention of the wrecking ball to take it apart.

On that first cable-laying attempt in 1865, one of the greatest captains to sail the blue sea was at the helm, Captain James Anderson. He really did manage not once, but numerous times, to find the one-inch cable when it was lost miles below on the ocean floor. Suspected sabotage by the Fenians is also recorded in the history books, and it was eventually discovered that the cable itself had done the damage when brittle shards of the outer casing imbedded themselves into the wire, shorting the signal.

The legend of the ghost aboard the *Great Eastern* is well documented in the ship's lore; and when the ship was finally dismantled, the skeletons of both the riveter and his bash boy were found between the hulls, where they had fallen to their deaths when the ship was being built. I have taken a little literary licence by naming these forgotten souls as their true identities have disappeared into the mists.

As a writer, I could not have dreamed up a more exciting plot. History itself has provided the people, setting and dramatic events complete with a ship of legend, ghosts, broken cables, storms, and sabotage. It is my hope that this book will instill in you a sense of wonder and respect for those intrepid scientists and explorers on whose inventions and discoveries our modern communications world is built. The next time you e-mail, text message or Twitter a friend, remember it all began long ago with a fragile thread thousands of miles long and those whispered "ghost messages."

GLOSSARY of NAUTICAL TERMS

Ahoy!: A very old and traditional greeting for hailing other vessels; originally a Viking battle cry.

Chewing the Fat: Having a long chat. "God made the vittles but the devil made the cook" was a popular saying used by seafaring men in the 19th century, when salted beef was the staple diet aboard ship. This tough cured beef, suitable only for long voyages when nothing else would keep (remember, there was no refrigeration) required prolonged chewing to make it edible. Men often chewed one chunk for hours, just as if it were chewing gum, and referred to this practice as "chewing the fat."

Devil to Pay or Paying the Devil: The expected unpleasant result of some action that has been taken. Sailors adopted the colourful idea of having to pay the devil for whatever fun you had and applied it to the most unpleasant tasks aboard a wooden ship. Caulking (sealing) seams and gaps in the ship was one of them: and it must certainly have been hellish to be suspended high above sea on the outside of a ship, or up to your knees in stinking bilgewater deep in the hold, using shredded rope and sticky black pitch to keep the saltwater out.

Fathom: A span of six feet. Fathom was originally a land-measuring term, derived from the Ango-Saxon word "faetm" meaning to embrace. In those days, most measurements were based on average size of parts of the body, such as the hand (horses are still measured this way) or the foot (that's why 12 inches are so named). A fathom was the average distance from fingertip to fingertip of the out-stretched arms of a man; or, as it was defined by an act of Parliament, "the length of a man's arms around the object of his affections."

Galley: The kitchen of a ship. It is most likely a corruption of "gallery." Ancient sailors cooked their meals on a brick or stone gallery laid amidships.

Head: The bathroom aboard a naval ship. The term comes from the days of sailing ships when the place for the crew to relieve themselves was all the way forward on either side of the bowsprit, the part of the hull to which the figure-head was fastened.

Holystone: A piece of sandstone used for scrubbing teak and other wooden decks. It was so nicknamed by an anonymous witty sailor because, as its use always brought a man to his knees, it must be holy!

Keelhauling: A naval punishment. A rope was passed under the bottom of the ship, and the punishee was attached to it, sometimes with weights attached to his legs. He was dropped suddenly into the sea on one side, hauled underneath the ship, and hoisted up on the other. When he had caught his breath, the punishment was repeated.

Pea Coat: A heavy topcoat worn in cold, miserable weather by seafaring men. Sailors who have to endure pea-soup weather often don their pea coats but the coat's name isn't derived from the weather. It was once tailored from pilot, or "P" cloth – a heavy, coarse, stout kind of twilled blue cloth. The garments made from it were called p-jackets or p-coats, later changed to pea jackets or peacoats.

Powder Monkey: Boys or young teens who carried bags of gunpowder from the powder magazine in the ship's hold to the gun crews aboard warships.

Scrimshaw: Carved or incised intricate designs on whalebone or whale ivory.

Scuttlebutt: Nautical parlance for gossip and rumour. In the navy, a water fountain is still called a "scuttlebutt," from the days when crews got their drinking water from a "scuttled butt" – a wooden cask (butt) that had a hole punched in for the water to flow through. (Sinking a ship by punching in its hull is called scuttling.) As they waited for their turn for a drink, crew members chatted and exchanged news, just like people still do at an office water cooler or school drinking fountain.

Sextant: A navigational instrument for determining latitude and longitude by measuring the angles of heavenly bodies in relation to the horizon.

S.O.S.: Contrary to popular notions, the letters S.O.S. do not stand for "Save Our Ship" or "Save Our Souls." They were selected to indicate distress because, in Morse code, these letters and their combination create an unmistakable sound pattern.

Starboard: The right side of a ship. The Vikings called the side of a ship its board, and they placed the steering oar or "star" on the right side. Because the oar was on the right side, the ship was tied to the dock at the left side. This was known as the loading side, or "larboard." Later, it was decided that "larboard" and "starboard" were too similar, especially when trying to be heard over the roar of a heavy sea, so larboard became the "side at which you tie up in port" or the "port" side.

Tar or Jack Tar: A slang term for a sailor. Early sailors wore overalls and broad-brimmed hats made of tar-impregnated fabric called tarpaulin cloth. The hats, and the sailors who wore them, were called tarpaulins, which may have been shortened to tars.

Watches: Divisions in a naval day. Traditionally, a 24-hour day is divided into seven watches. These are: midnight to 4 a.m., mid-watch; 4 to 8 a.m., morning watch; 8 a.m. to noon, forenoon watch; noon to 4 p.m., afternoon watch; 4 to 6 p.m., first dogwatch; 6 to 8 p.m., second dogwatch; and, 8 p.m. to midnight, evening watch. The half-hours of the watch are marked by striking the bell an appropriate number of times.

MORSE CODE ALPHABET

A	.-	O	---	2	..---
B	-...	P	.--.	3	...--
C	-.-.	Q	--.-	4	....-
D	-..	R	.-.	5	.....
E	.	S	...	6	-....
F	..-.	T	-	7	--...
G	--.	U	..-	8	---..
H	....	V	...-	9	----.
I	..	W	.--	Fullstop	.-.-.-
J	.---	X	-..-	Comma	--..--
K	-.-	Y	-.--	Query	..--..
L	.-..	Z	--..		
M	--	0	-----		
N	-.	1	.----		

ACKNOWLEDGEMENTS

I would like to thank Nik Burton of Coteau Books for giving me the opportunity to bring a fun book to life and Ms. Laura Peetoom for being the editor of my dreams!

The author wishes to acknowledge the Alberta Foundation for the Arts for their kind support in the writing of this book.

ABOUT the AUTHOR

Jacqueline Guest is the author of more than a dozen books for young readers, specializing in sports themes or historical fiction. Her books have received numerous Our Choice and Young Readers Choice citations. Jacqueline Guest lives and writes in the Rocky Mountain foothills of Alberta.